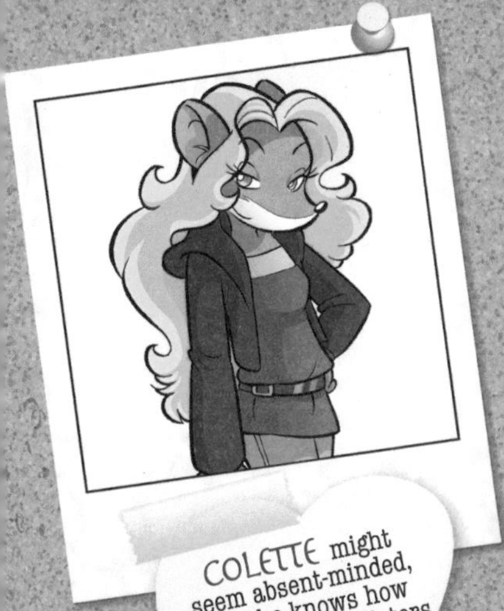

COLETTE might seem absent-minded, but she knows how to get the Thea Sisters out of trouble when she needs to.

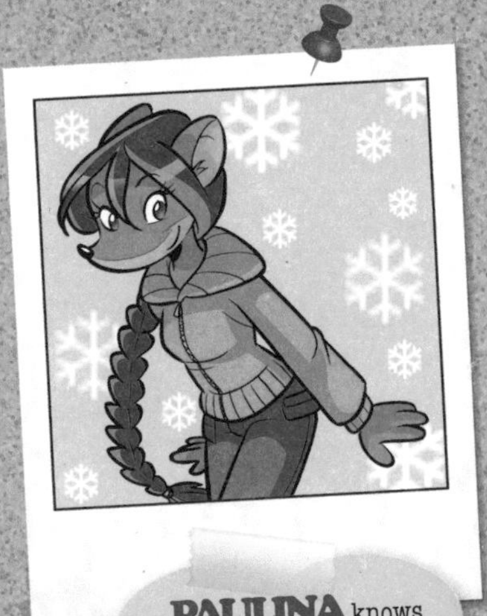

PAULINA knows how to surf the web like no one else. With her laptop, she can find any information she needs on the Internet.

Here's the **Whale Island** port! It's where all the ships embark from, even those heading towards Mouse Island.

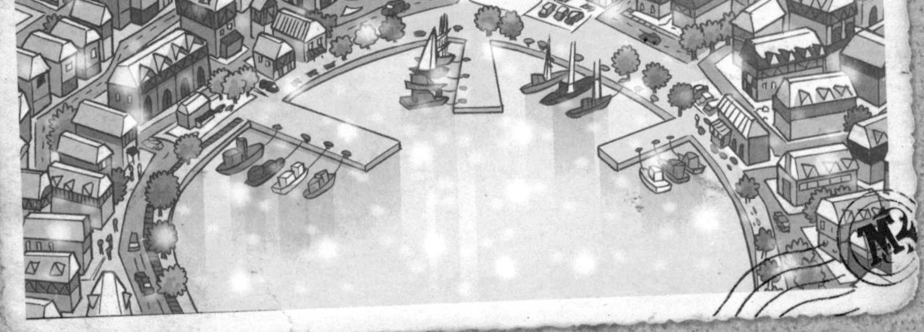

Thea Stilton

PAPERCUTZ™

Thea Stilton

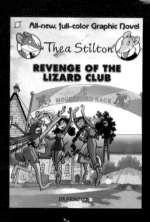

Thea Stilton
THE TREASURE OF THE VIKING SHIP
By Thea Stilton

PAPERCUTZ™

THE TREASURE OF THE VIKING SHIP
© EDIZIONI PIEMME 2009 S.p.A.
Corso Como 15, 20145,
Milan, Italy
Geronimo Stilton and Thea Stilton names, characters and related indicia are copyright,
trademark and exclusive license of Atlantyca S.p.A.
All rights reserved.
The moral right of the author has been asserted.

Text by Thea Stilton
Text Coordination by Lorenza Bernardi and Sarah Rossi (Atlantyca S.p.A.)
Editorial coordination by Patrizia Puricelli and Serena Bellani
Artistic Coordination by Flavio Ferron
With the assistance of Tommaso Valsechi
Editing by Yellowhale
Editing Coordination and Artwork Supervision by Stefania Bitta and Maryam Funicelli
Script Supervision by Francesco Artibani
Script by Francesco Artibani and Caterina Mognato
Design by Claudia Forcelloni
Art by Michela Frare
Color by Giulia Basile, Alessandra Bracaglia, and Vanessa Santato
With the assistance of Michela Battaglin and Marta Lorini
Cover by Claudia Forcelloni (design), Michela Frare (art), and Guilia Basile (color)

Based on an original idea by Elisabetta Dami
© 2014 – for this work in English language by Papercutz.
Original title: "Il Tesoro Della Nave Vichinga"
Translation by: Nanette McGuinness
www.geronimostilton.com

Stilton is the name of a famous English cheese. It is a registered trademark of the
Stilton Cheese Makers' Association. For more information go to www.stiltoncheese.com

Papercutz books may be purchased for business or promotional use. For information on bulk purchases
please contact Macmillan Corporate and Premium Sales Department at (800) 221-7945 x5442.

Lettering and Production -- Big Bird Zatryb
Production Coordinator -- Beth Scorzato
Editor -- Michael Petranek
Jim Salicrup
Editor-in-Chief

ISBN: 978-1-59707-514-5

Printed in China.
March 2016 by WKT Co. LTD.
3/F Phase 1 Leader Industrial Centre
188 Texaco Road, Tsuen Wan, N.T.
Hong Kong

Distributed by Macmillan
Second Papercutz Printing

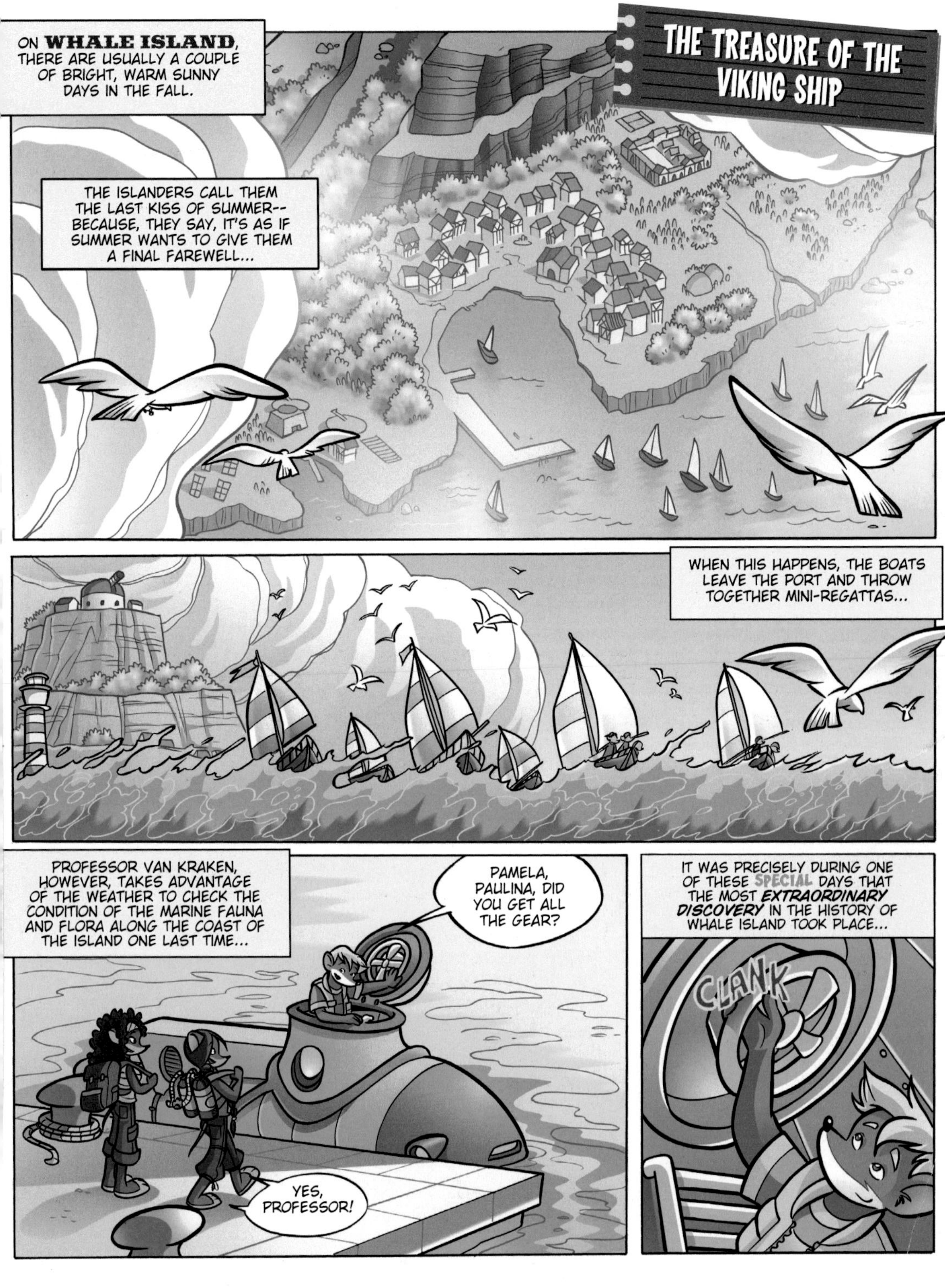
ON WHALE ISLAND, THERE ARE USUALLY A COUPLE OF BRIGHT, WARM SUNNY DAYS IN THE FALL.
THE TREASURE OF THE VIKING SHIP
THE ISLANDERS CALL THEM THE LAST KISS OF SUMMER-- BECAUSE, THEY SAY, IT'S AS IF SUMMER WANTS TO GIVE THEM A FINAL FAREWELL...
WHEN THIS HAPPENS, THE BOATS LEAVE THE PORT AND THROW TOGETHER MINI-REGATTAS...
PROFESSOR VAN KRAKEN, HOWEVER, TAKES ADVANTAGE OF THE WEATHER TO CHECK THE CONDITION OF THE MARINE FAUNA AND FLORA ALONG THE COAST OF THE ISLAND ONE LAST TIME...
PAMELA, PAULINA, DID YOU GET ALL THE GEAR?
YES, PROFESSOR!
IT WAS PRECISELY DURING ONE OF THESE SPECIAL DAYS THAT THE MOST EXTRAORDINARY DISCOVERY IN THE HISTORY OF WHALE ISLAND TOOK PLACE...
CLANK

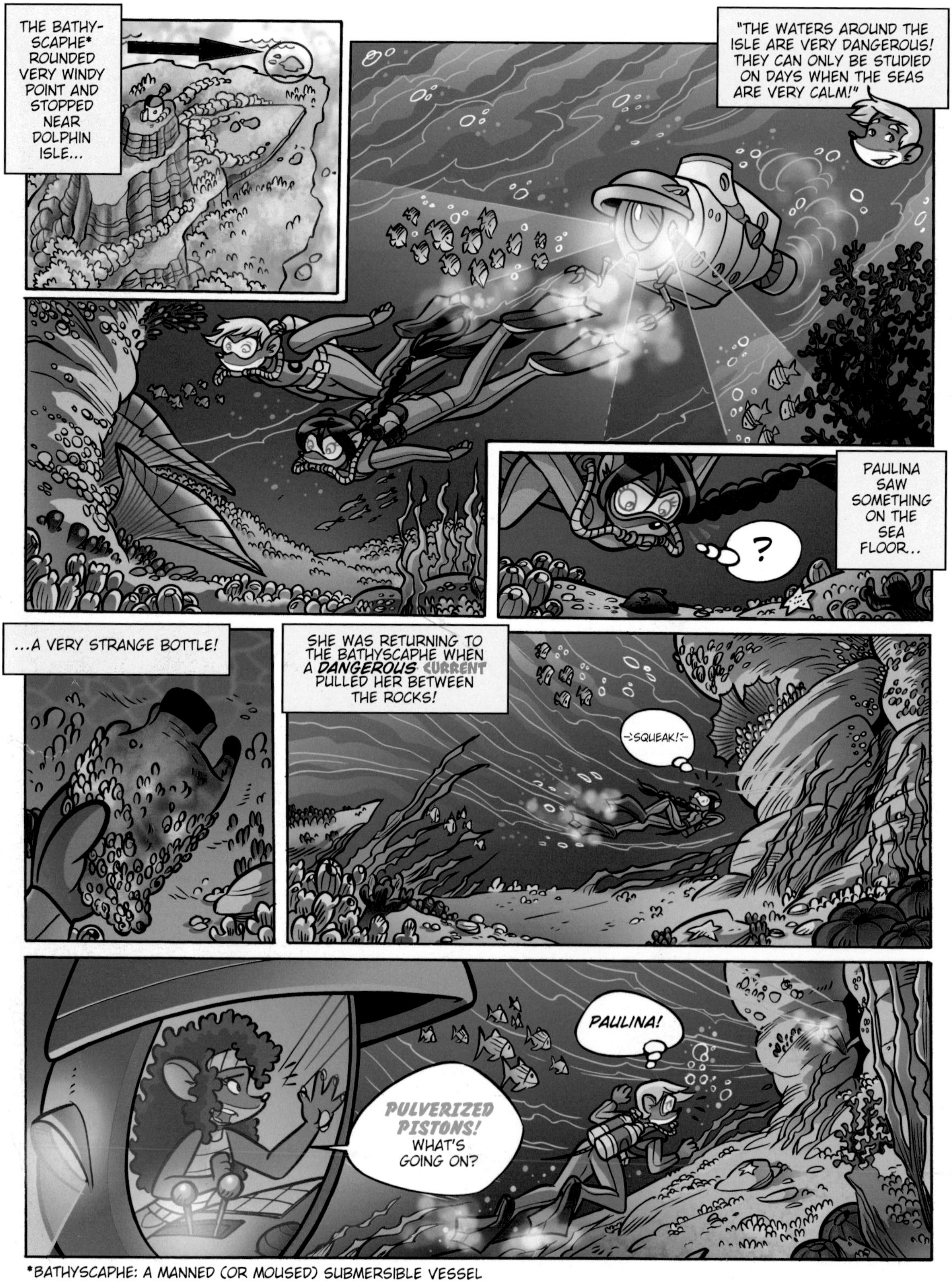
THE BATHY-SCAPHE* ROUNDED VERY WINDY POINT AND STOPPED NEAR DOLPHIN ISLE...
"THE WATERS AROUND THE ISLE ARE VERY DANGEROUS! THEY CAN ONLY BE STUDIED ON DAYS WHEN THE SEAS ARE VERY CALM!"
PAULINA SAW SOMETHING ON THE SEA FLOOR...
?
...A VERY STRANGE BOTTLE!
SHE WAS RETURNING TO THE BATHYSCAPHE WHEN A DANGEROUS CURRENT PULLED HER BETWEEN THE ROCKS!
SQUEAK!
PAULINA!
PULVERIZED PISTONS! WHAT'S GOING ON?

*BATHYSCAPHE: A MANNED (OR MOUSED) SUBMERSIBLE VESSEL

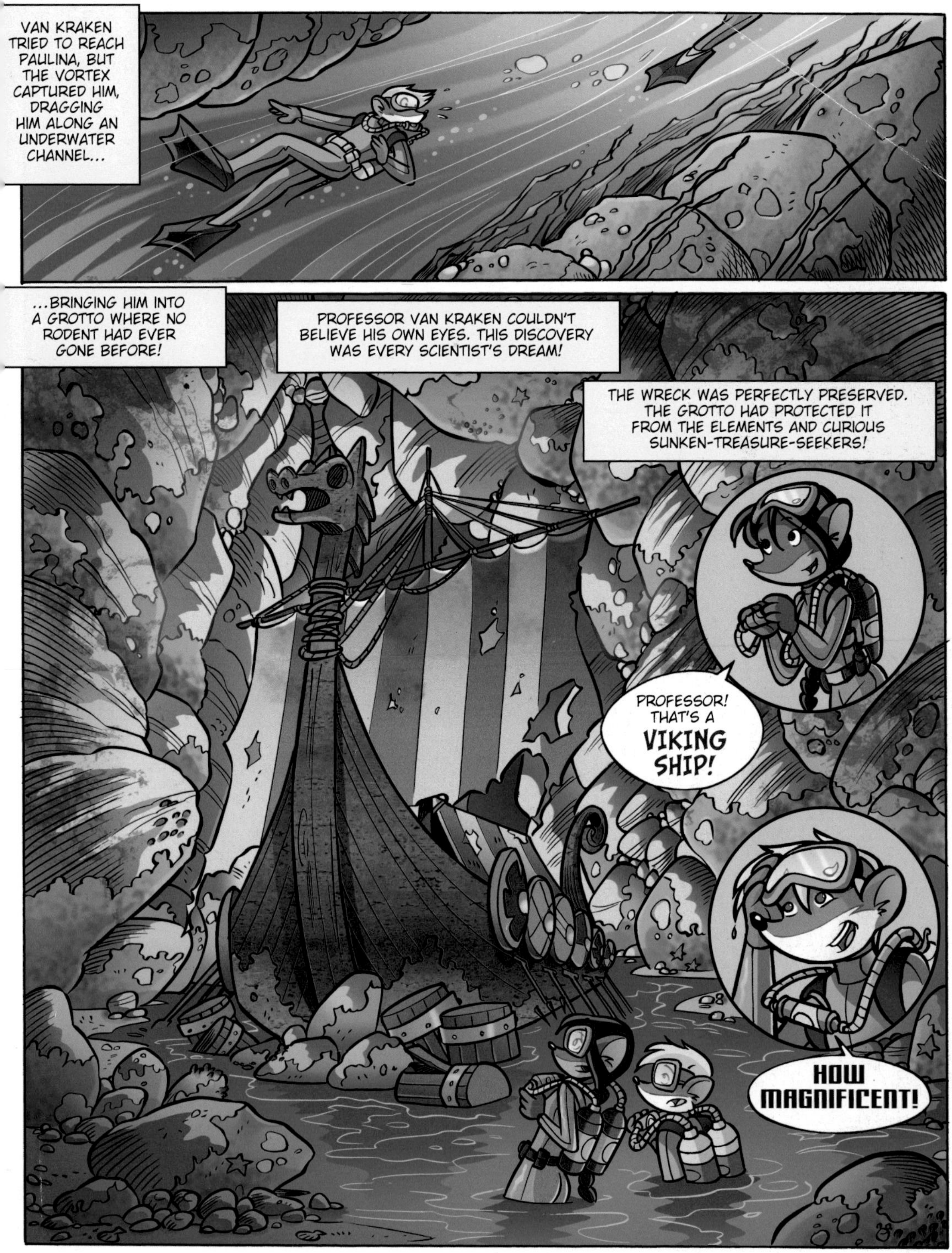
VAN KRAKEN TRIED TO REACH PAULINA, BUT THE VORTEX CAPTURED HIM, DRAGGING HIM ALONG AN UNDERWATER CHANNEL...
...BRINGING HIM INTO A GROTTO WHERE NO RODENT HAD EVER GONE BEFORE!
PROFESSOR VAN KRAKEN COULDN'T BELIEVE HIS OWN EYES. THIS DISCOVERY WAS EVERY SCIENTIST'S DREAM!
THE WRECK WAS PERFECTLY PRESERVED. THE GROTTO HAD PROTECTED IT FROM THE ELEMENTS AND CURIOUS SUNKEN-TREASURE-SEEKERS!
PROFESSOR! THAT'S A VIKING SHIP!
HOW MAGNIFICENT!

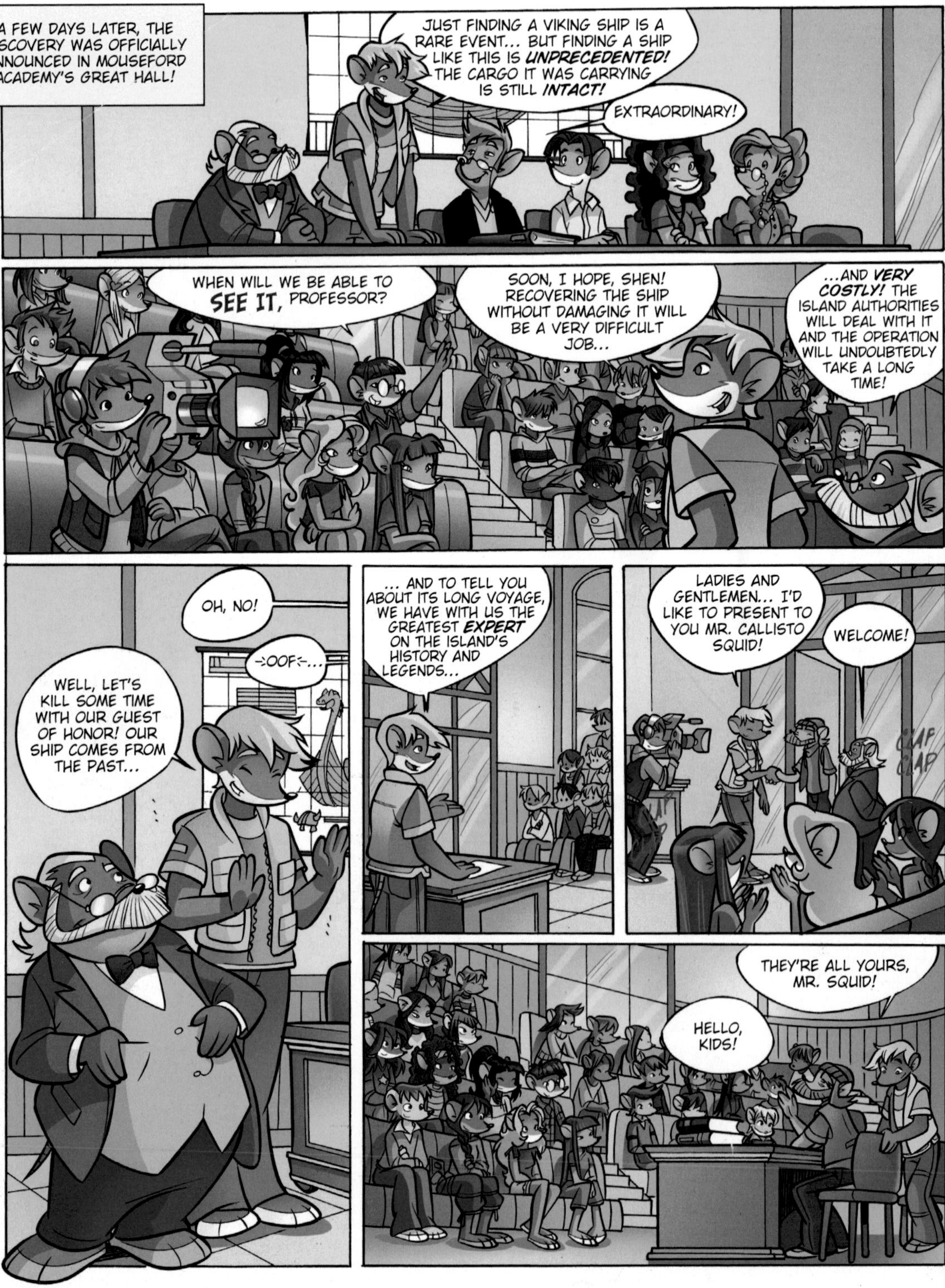
A FEW DAYS LATER, THE DISCOVERY WAS OFFICIALLY ANNOUNCED IN MOUSEFORD ACADEMY'S GREAT HALL!
JUST FINDING A VIKING SHIP IS A RARE EVENT... BUT FINDING A SHIP LIKE THIS IS UNPRECEDENTED! THE CARGO IT WAS CARRYING IS STILL INTACT!
EXTRAORDINARY!
WHEN WILL WE BE ABLE TO SEE IT, PROFESSOR?
SOON, I HOPE, SHEN! RECOVERING THE SHIP WITHOUT DAMAGING IT WILL BE A VERY DIFFICULT JOB...
...AND VERY COSTLY! THE ISLAND AUTHORITIES WILL DEAL WITH IT AND THE OPERATION WILL UNDOUBTEDLY TAKE A LONG TIME!
OH, NO!
>OOF<...
WELL, LET'S KILL SOME TIME WITH OUR GUEST OF HONOR! OUR SHIP COMES FROM THE PAST...
... AND TO TELL YOU ABOUT ITS LONG VOYAGE, WE HAVE WITH US THE GREATEST EXPERT ON THE ISLAND'S HISTORY AND LEGENDS...
LADIES AND GENTLEMEN... I'D LIKE TO PRESENT TO YOU MR. CALLISTO SQUID!
WELCOME!
CLAP CLAP
THEY'RE ALL YOURS, MR. SQUID!
HELLO, KIDS!

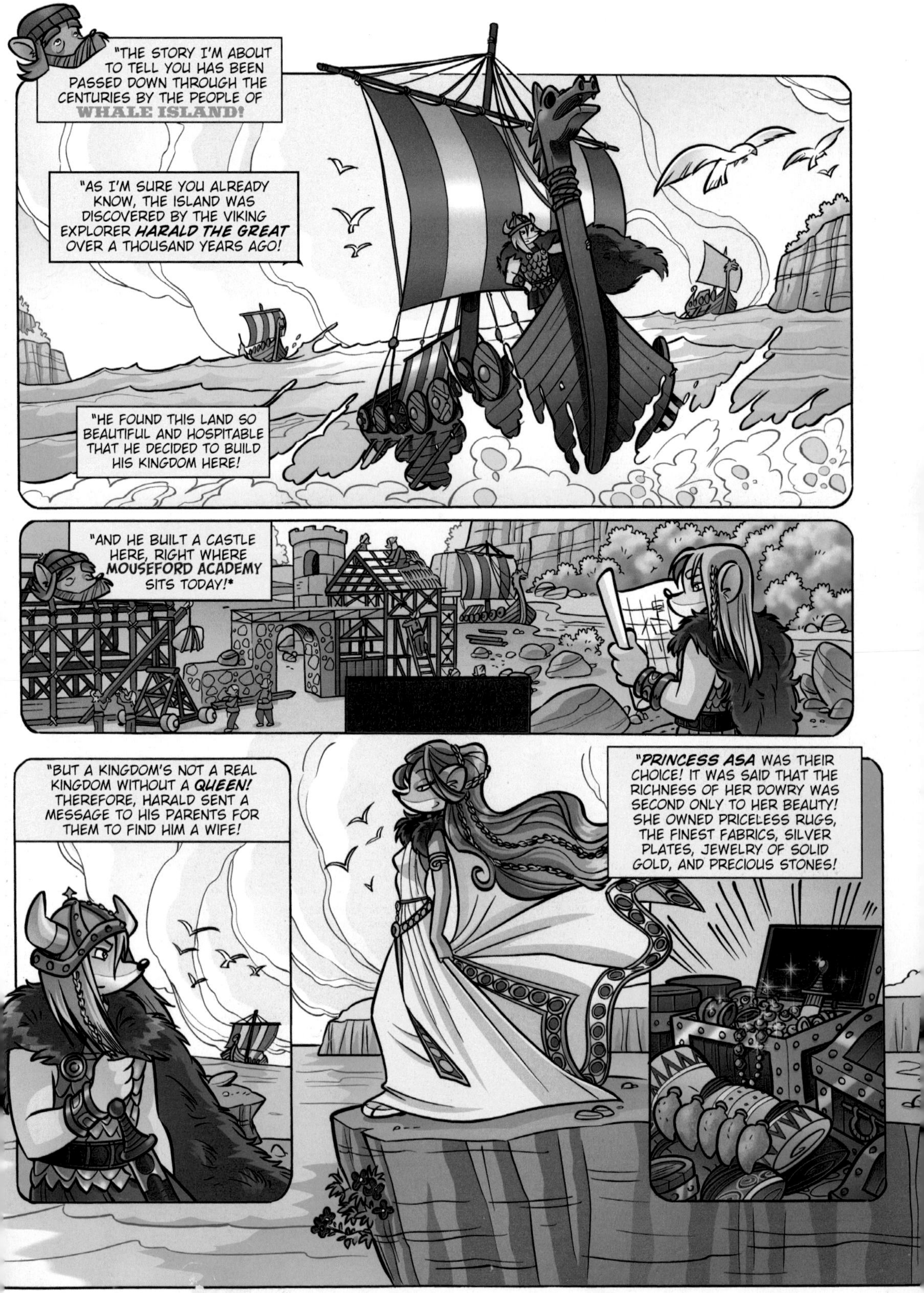
"THE STORY I'M ABOUT TO TELL YOU HAS BEEN PASSED DOWN THROUGH THE CENTURIES BY THE PEOPLE OF WHALE ISLAND!
"AS I'M SURE YOU ALREADY KNOW, THE ISLAND WAS DISCOVERED BY THE VIKING EXPLORER HARALD THE GREAT OVER A THOUSAND YEARS AGO!
"HE FOUND THIS LAND SO BEAUTIFUL AND HOSPITABLE THAT HE DECIDED TO BUILD HIS KINGDOM HERE!
"AND HE BUILT A CASTLE HERE, RIGHT WHERE MOUSEFORD ACADEMY SITS TODAY!*
[redacted]
"BUT A KINGDOM'S NOT A REAL KINGDOM WITHOUT A QUEEN! THEREFORE, HARALD SENT A MESSAGE TO HIS PARENTS FOR THEM TO FIND HIM A WIFE!
"PRINCESS ASA WAS THEIR CHOICE! IT WAS SAID THAT THE RICHNESS OF HER DOWRY WAS SECOND ONLY TO HER BEAUTY! SHE OWNED PRICELESS RUGS, THE FINEST FABRICS, SILVER PLATES, JEWELRY OF SOLID GOLD, AND PRECIOUS STONES!

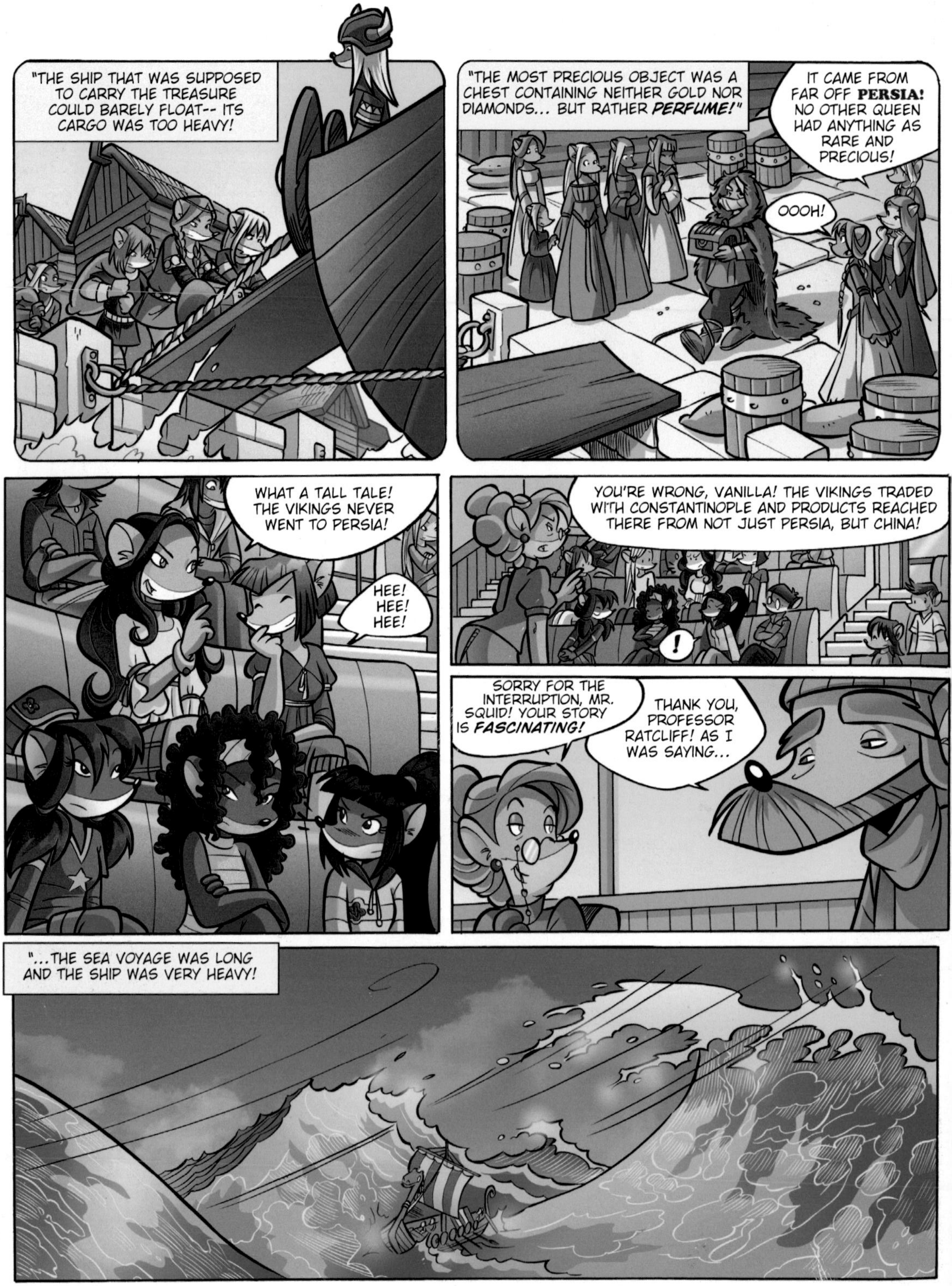
"THE SHIP THAT WAS SUPPOSED TO CARRY THE TREASURE COULD BARELY FLOAT-- ITS CARGO WAS TOO HEAVY!
"THE MOST PRECIOUS OBJECT WAS A CHEST CONTAINING NEITHER GOLD NOR DIAMONDS... BUT RATHER PERFUME!"
IT CAME FROM FAR OFF PERSIA! NO OTHER QUEEN HAD ANYTHING AS RARE AND PRECIOUS!
OOOH!
WHAT A TALL TALE! THE VIKINGS NEVER WENT TO PERSIA!
HEE! HEE! HEE!
YOU'RE WRONG, VANILLA! THE VIKINGS TRADED WITH CONSTANTINOPLE AND PRODUCTS REACHED THERE FROM NOT JUST PERSIA, BUT CHINA!
!
SORRY FOR THE INTERRUPTION, MR. SQUID! YOUR STORY IS FASCINATING!
THANK YOU, PROFESSOR RATCLIFF! AS I WAS SAYING...
"...THE SEA VOYAGE WAS LONG AND THE SHIP WAS VERY HEAVY!

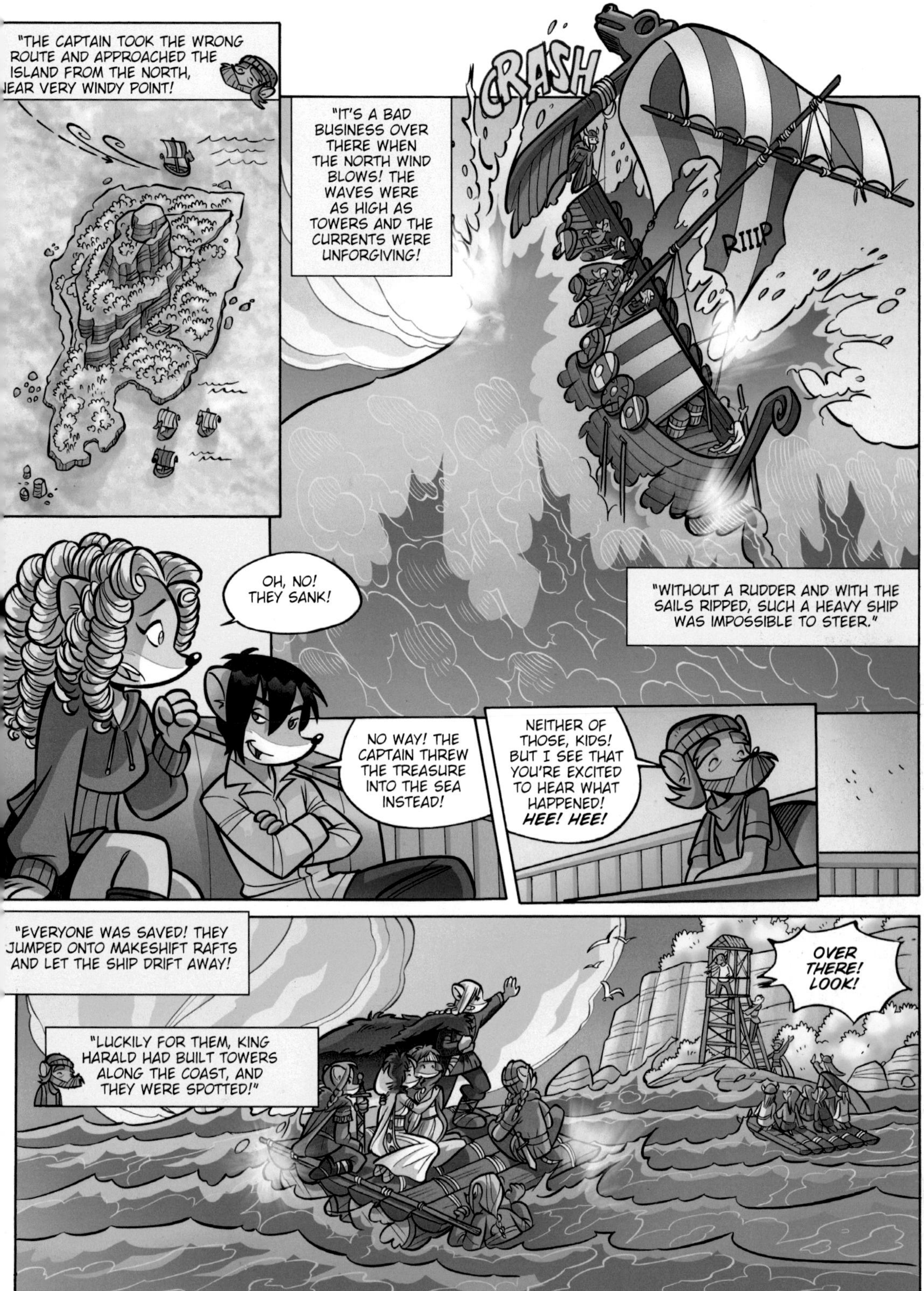
"THE CAPTAIN TOOK THE WRONG ROUTE AND APPROACHED THE ISLAND FROM THE NORTH, NEAR VERY WINDY POINT!
"IT'S A BAD BUSINESS OVER THERE WHEN THE NORTH WIND BLOWS! THE WAVES WERE AS HIGH AS TOWERS AND THE CURRENTS WERE UNFORGIVING!
CRASH
RIIIP
"WITHOUT A RUDDER AND WITH THE SAILS RIPPED, SUCH A HEAVY SHIP WAS IMPOSSIBLE TO STEER."
OH, NO! THEY SANK!
NO WAY! THE CAPTAIN THREW THE TREASURE INTO THE SEA INSTEAD!
NEITHER OF THOSE, KIDS! BUT I SEE THAT YOU'RE EXCITED TO HEAR WHAT HAPPENED! HEE! HEE!
"EVERYONE WAS SAVED! THEY JUMPED ONTO MAKESHIFT RAFTS AND LET THE SHIP DRIFT AWAY!
"LUCKILY FOR THEM, KING HARALD HAD BUILT TOWERS ALONG THE COAST, AND THEY WERE SPOTTED!"
OVER THERE! LOOK!

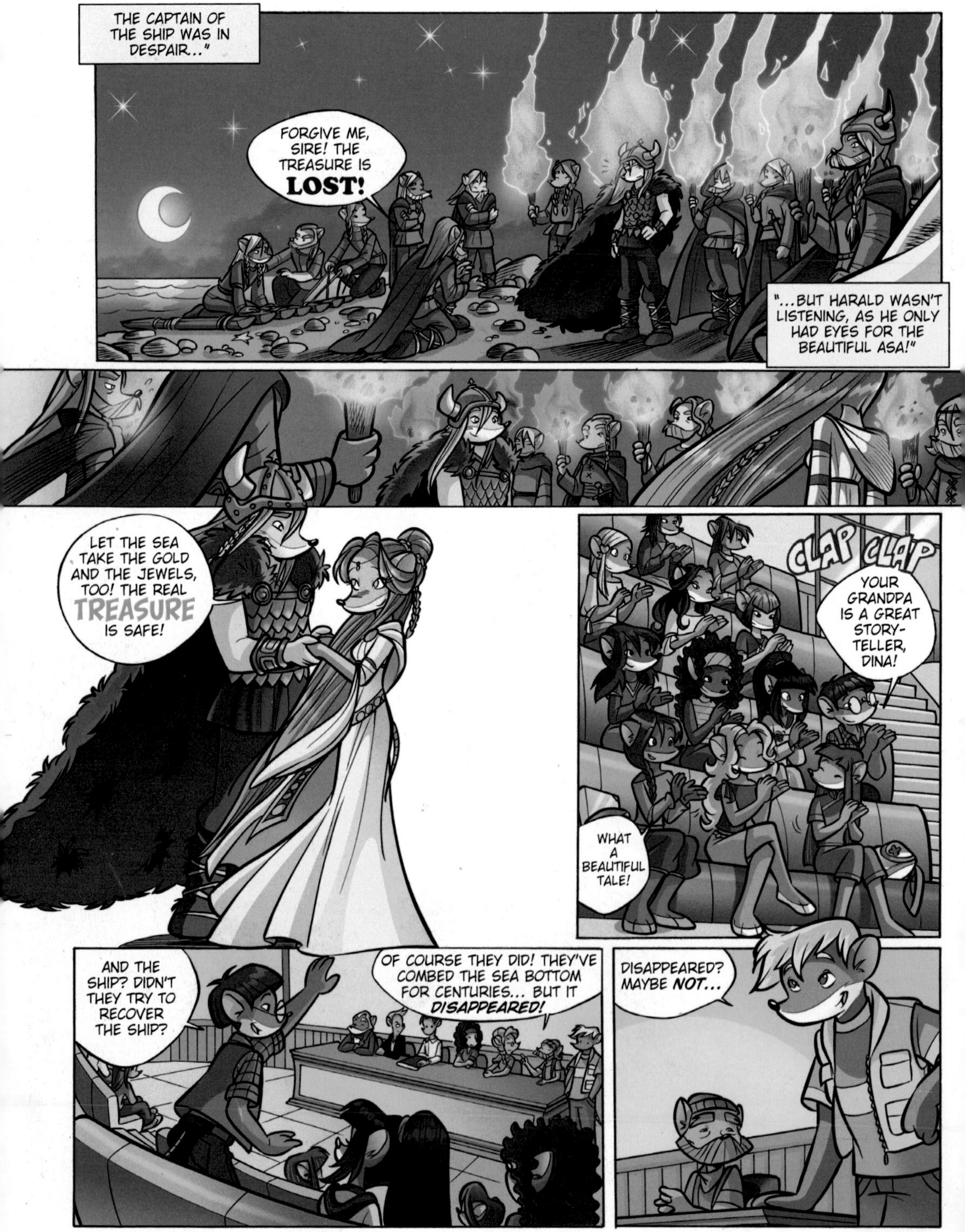
THE CAPTAIN OF THE SHIP WAS IN DESPAIR..."
FORGIVE ME, SIRE! THE TREASURE IS LOST!
"...BUT HARALD WASN'T LISTENING, AS HE ONLY HAD EYES FOR THE BEAUTIFUL ASA!"
LET THE SEA TAKE THE GOLD AND THE JEWELS, TOO! THE REAL TREASURE IS SAFE!
CLAP CLAP
YOUR GRANDPA IS A GREAT STORY-TELLER, DINA!
WHAT A BEAUTIFUL TALE!
AND THE SHIP? DIDN'T THEY TRY TO RECOVER THE SHIP?
OF COURSE THEY DID! THEY'VE COMBED THE SEA BOTTOM FOR CENTURIES... BUT IT DISAPPEARED!
DISAPPEARED? MAYBE NOT...

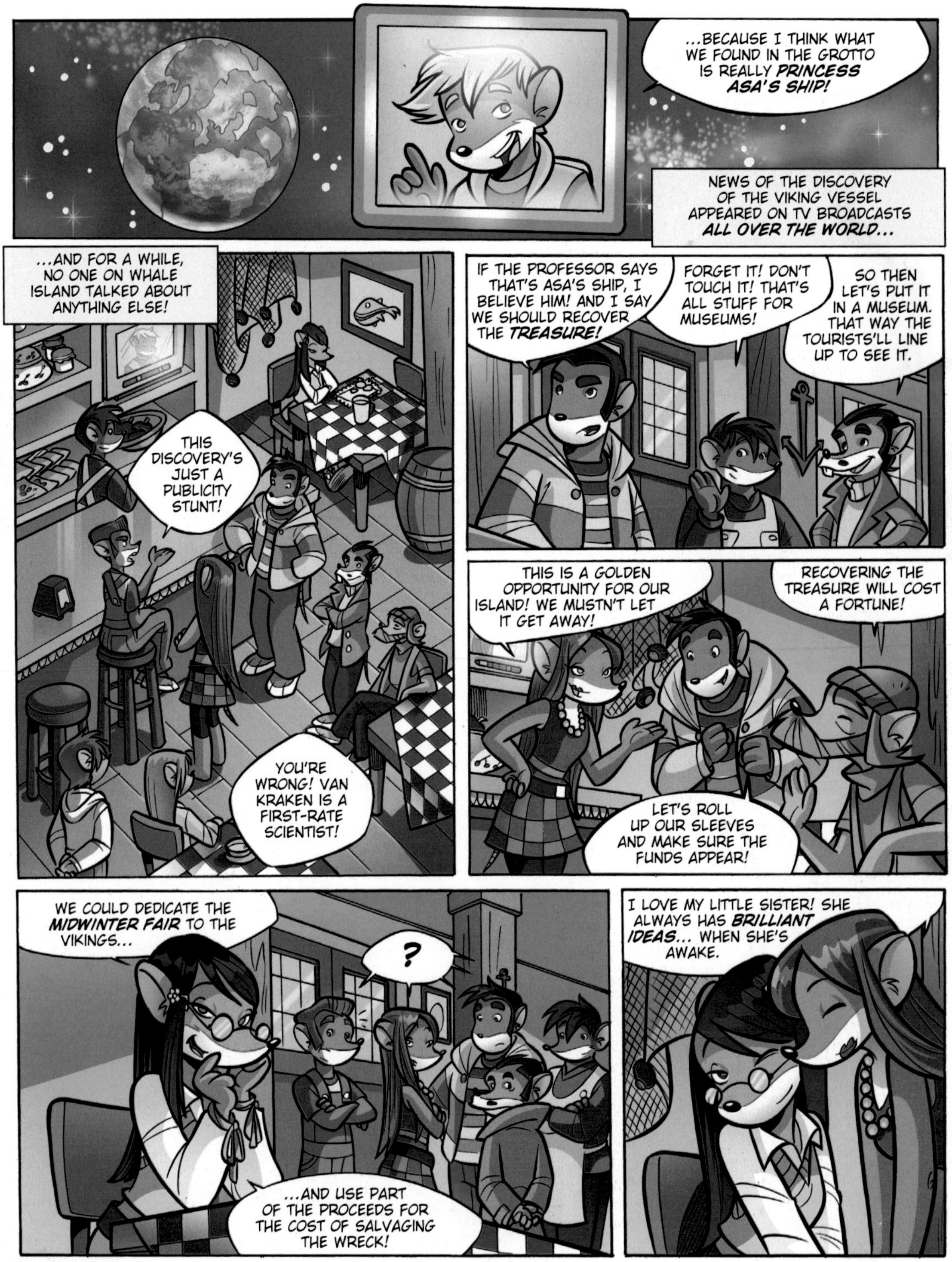
...BECAUSE I THINK WHAT WE FOUND IN THE GROTTO IS REALLY PRINCESS ASA'S SHIP!
NEWS OF THE DISCOVERY OF THE VIKING VESSEL APPEARED ON TV BROADCASTS ALL OVER THE WORLD...
...AND FOR A WHILE, NO ONE ON WHALE ISLAND TALKED ABOUT ANYTHING ELSE!
THIS DISCOVERY'S JUST A PUBLICITY STUNT!
YOU'RE WRONG! VAN KRAKEN IS A FIRST-RATE SCIENTIST!
IF THE PROFESSOR SAYS THAT'S ASA'S SHIP, I BELIEVE HIM! AND I SAY WE SHOULD RECOVER THE TREASURE!
FORGET IT! DON'T TOUCH IT! THAT'S ALL STUFF FOR MUSEUMS!
SO THEN LET'S PUT IT IN A MUSEUM. THAT WAY THE TOURISTS'LL LINE UP TO SEE IT.
THIS IS A GOLDEN OPPORTUNITY FOR OUR ISLAND! WE MUSTN'T LET IT GET AWAY!
RECOVERING THE TREASURE WILL COST A FORTUNE!
LET'S ROLL UP OUR SLEEVES AND MAKE SURE THE FUNDS APPEAR!
WE COULD DEDICATE THE MIDWINTER FAIR TO THE VIKINGS...
?
...AND USE PART OF THE PROCEEDS FOR THE COST OF SALVAGING THE WRECK!
I LOVE MY LITTLE SISTER! SHE ALWAYS HAS BRILLIANT IDEAS... WHEN SHE'S AWAKE.

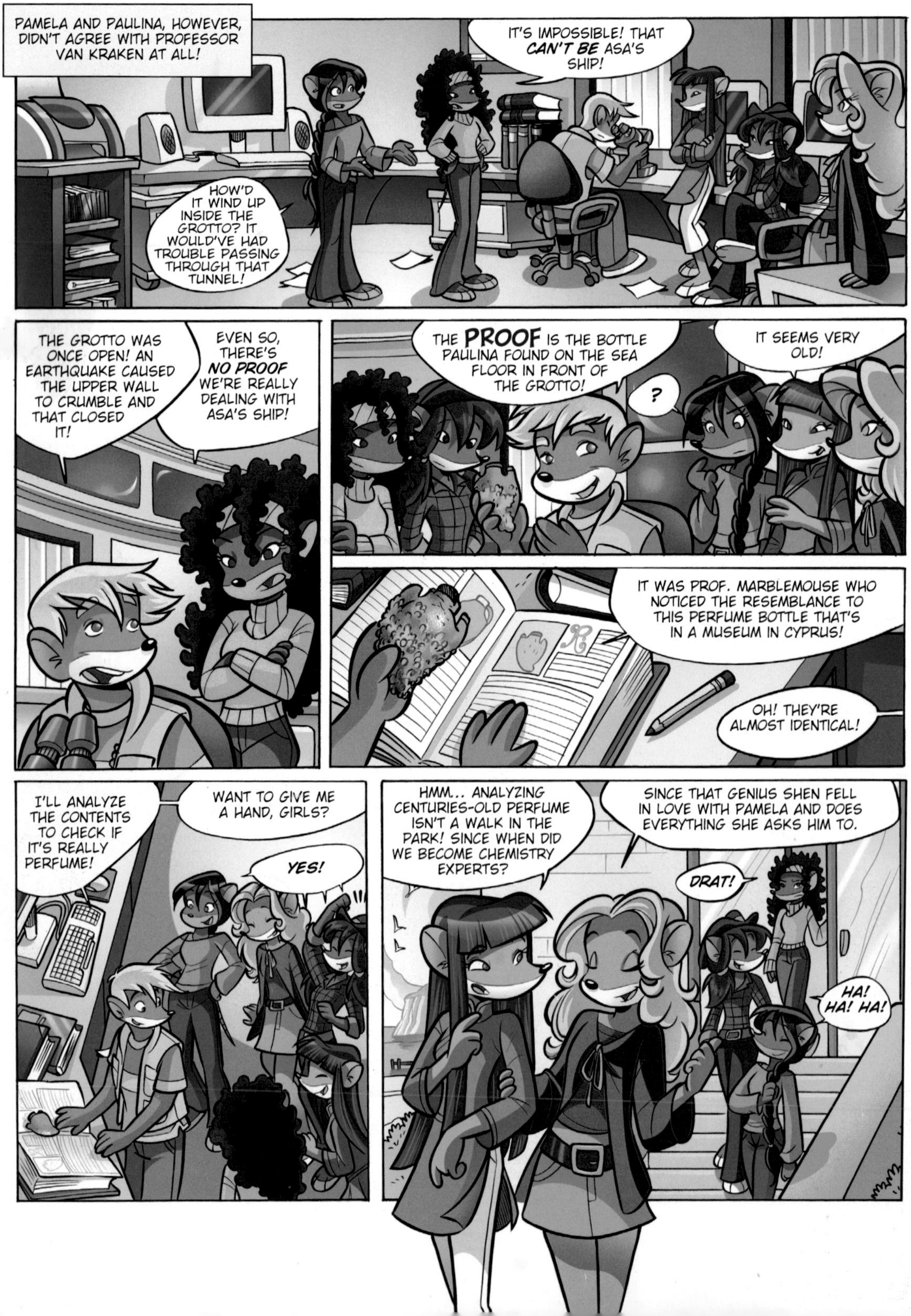

PAMELA AND PAULINA, HOWEVER, DIDN'T AGREE WITH PROFESSOR VAN KRAKEN AT ALL!
IT'S IMPOSSIBLE! THAT CAN'T BE ASA'S SHIP!
HOW'D IT WIND UP INSIDE THE GROTTO? IT WOULD'VE HAD TROUBLE PASSING THROUGH THAT TUNNEL!
THE GROTTO WAS ONCE OPEN! AN EARTHQUAKE CAUSED THE UPPER WALL TO CRUMBLE AND THAT CLOSED IT!
EVEN SO, THERE'S NO PROOF WE'RE REALLY DEALING WITH ASA'S SHIP!
THE PROOF IS THE BOTTLE PAULINA FOUND ON THE SEA FLOOR IN FRONT OF THE GROTTO!
?
IT SEEMS VERY OLD!
IT WAS PROF. MARBLEMOUSE WHO NOTICED THE RESEMBLANCE TO THIS PERFUME BOTTLE THAT'S IN A MUSEUM IN CYPRUS!
OH! THEY'RE ALMOST IDENTICAL!
I'LL ANALYZE THE CONTENTS TO CHECK IF IT'S REALLY PERFUME!
WANT TO GIVE ME A HAND, GIRLS?
YES!
HMM... ANALYZING CENTURIES-OLD PERFUME ISN'T A WALK IN THE PARK! SINCE WHEN DID WE BECOME CHEMISTRY EXPERTS?
SINCE THAT GENIUS SHEN FELL IN LOVE WITH PAMELA AND DOES EVERYTHING SHE ASKS HIM TO.
DRAT!
HA! HA! HA!

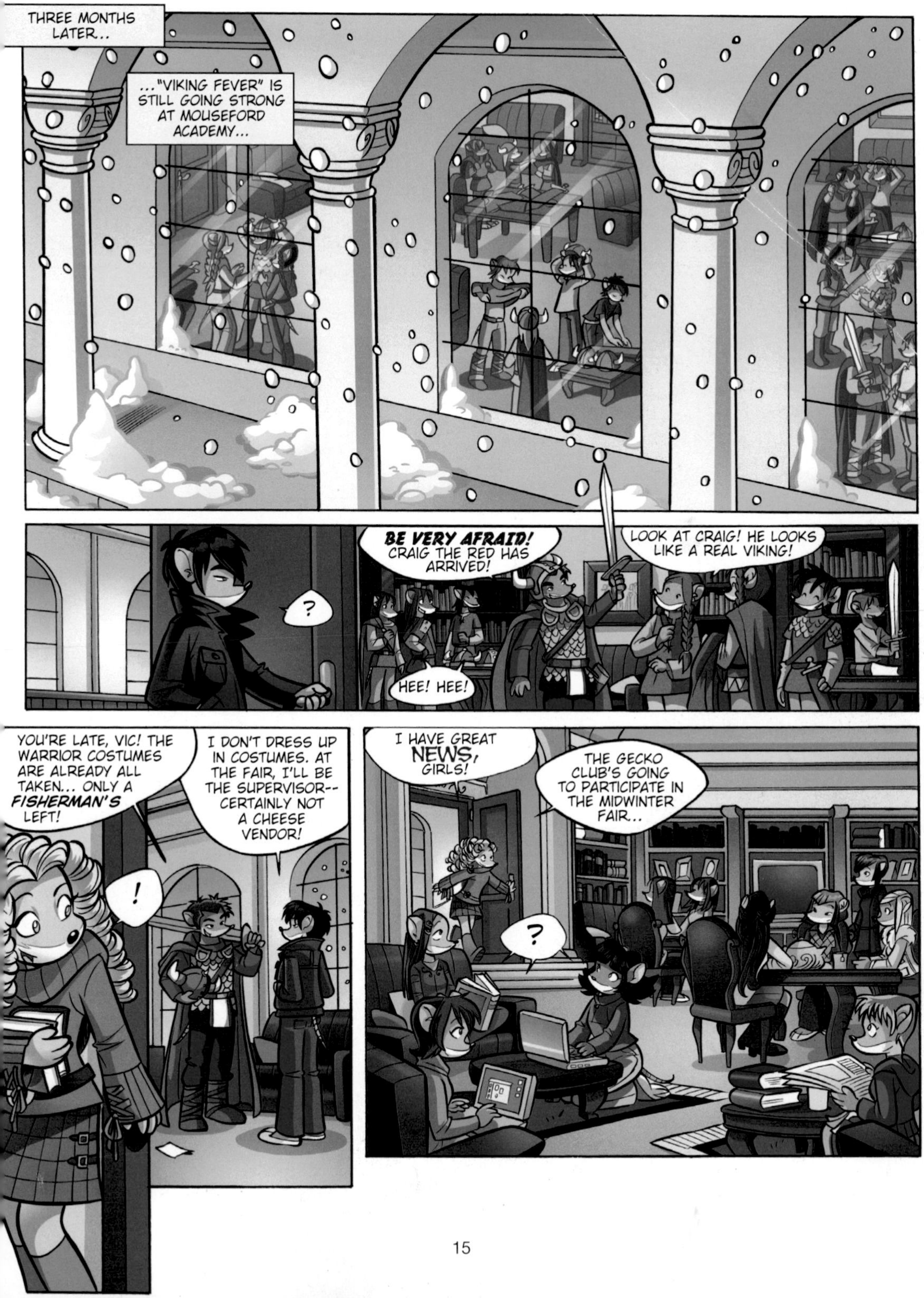
THREE MONTHS LATER...
..."VIKING FEVER" IS STILL GOING STRONG AT MOUSEFORD ACADEMY...
?
BE VERY AFRAID! CRAIG THE RED HAS ARRIVED!
HEE! HEE!
LOOK AT CRAIG! HE LOOKS LIKE A REAL VIKING!
YOU'RE LATE, VIC! THE WARRIOR COSTUMES ARE ALREADY ALL TAKEN... ONLY A FISHERMAN'S LEFT!
I DON'T DRESS UP IN COSTUMES. AT THE FAIR, I'LL BE THE SUPERVISOR-- CERTAINLY NOT A CHEESE VENDOR!
!
I HAVE GREAT NEWS, GIRLS!
THE GECKO CLUB'S GOING TO PARTICIPATE IN THE MIDWINTER FAIR...
?

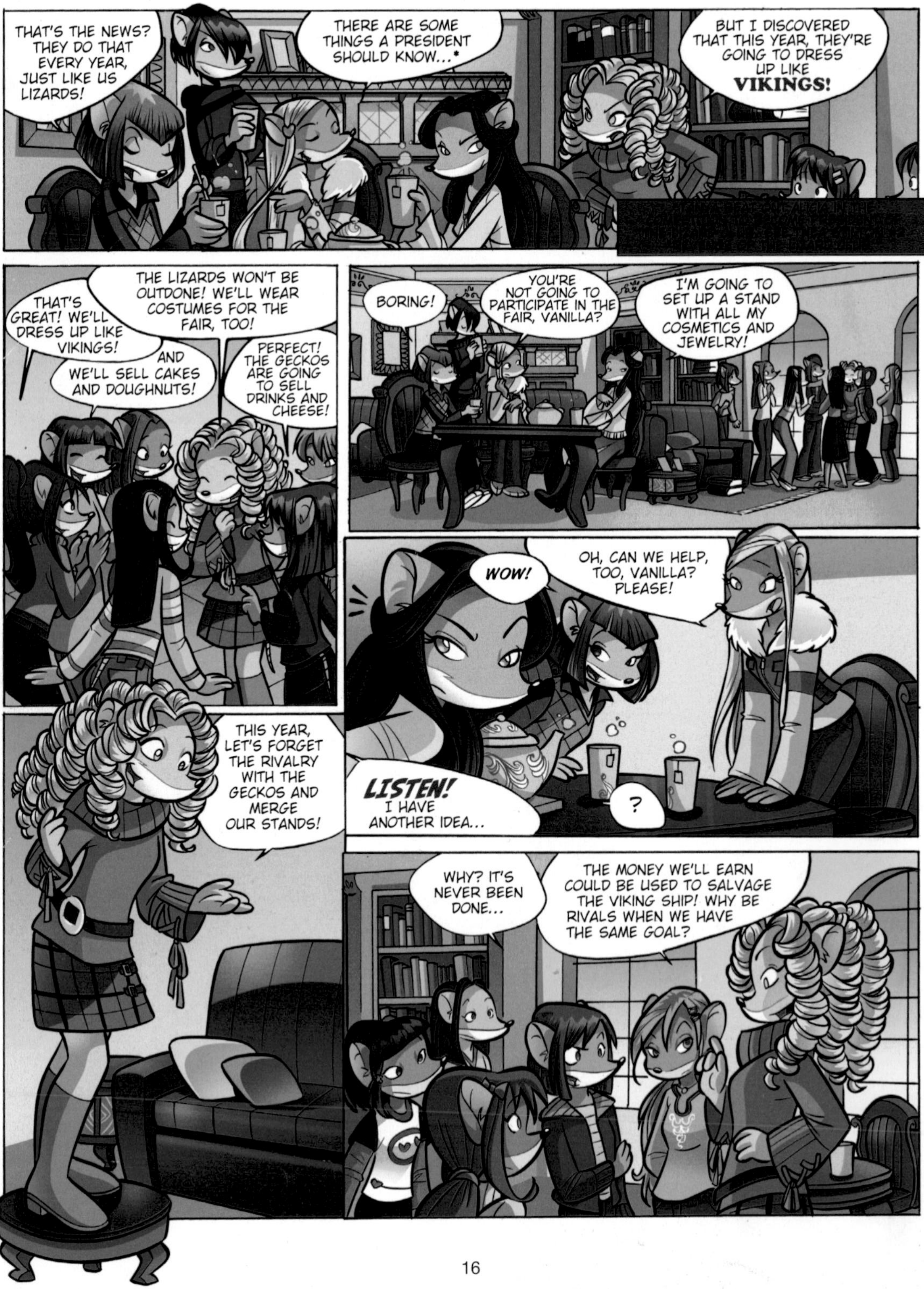
THAT'S THE NEWS? THEY DO THAT EVERY YEAR, JUST LIKE US LIZARDS!
THERE ARE SOME THINGS A PRESIDENT SHOULD KNOW...*
BUT I DISCOVERED THAT THIS YEAR, THEY'RE GOING TO DRESS UP LIKE VIKINGS!
[redacted]
THAT'S GREAT! WE'LL DRESS UP LIKE VIKINGS!
THE LIZARDS WON'T BE OUTDONE! WE'LL WEAR COSTUMES FOR THE FAIR, TOO!
AND WE'LL SELL CAKES AND DOUGHNUTS!
PERFECT! THE GECKOS ARE GOING TO SELL DRINKS AND CHEESE!
BORING!
YOU'RE NOT GOING TO PARTICIPATE IN THE FAIR, VANILLA?
I'M GOING TO SET UP A STAND WITH ALL MY COSMETICS AND JEWELRY!
WOW!
OH, CAN WE HELP, TOO, VANILLA? PLEASE!
LISTEN! I HAVE ANOTHER IDEA...
?
THIS YEAR, LET'S FORGET THE RIVALRY WITH THE GECKOS AND MERGE OUR STANDS!
WHY? IT'S NEVER BEEN DONE...
THE MONEY WE'LL EARN COULD BE USED TO SALVAGE THE VIKING SHIP! WHY BE RIVALS WHEN WE HAVE THE SAME GOAL?

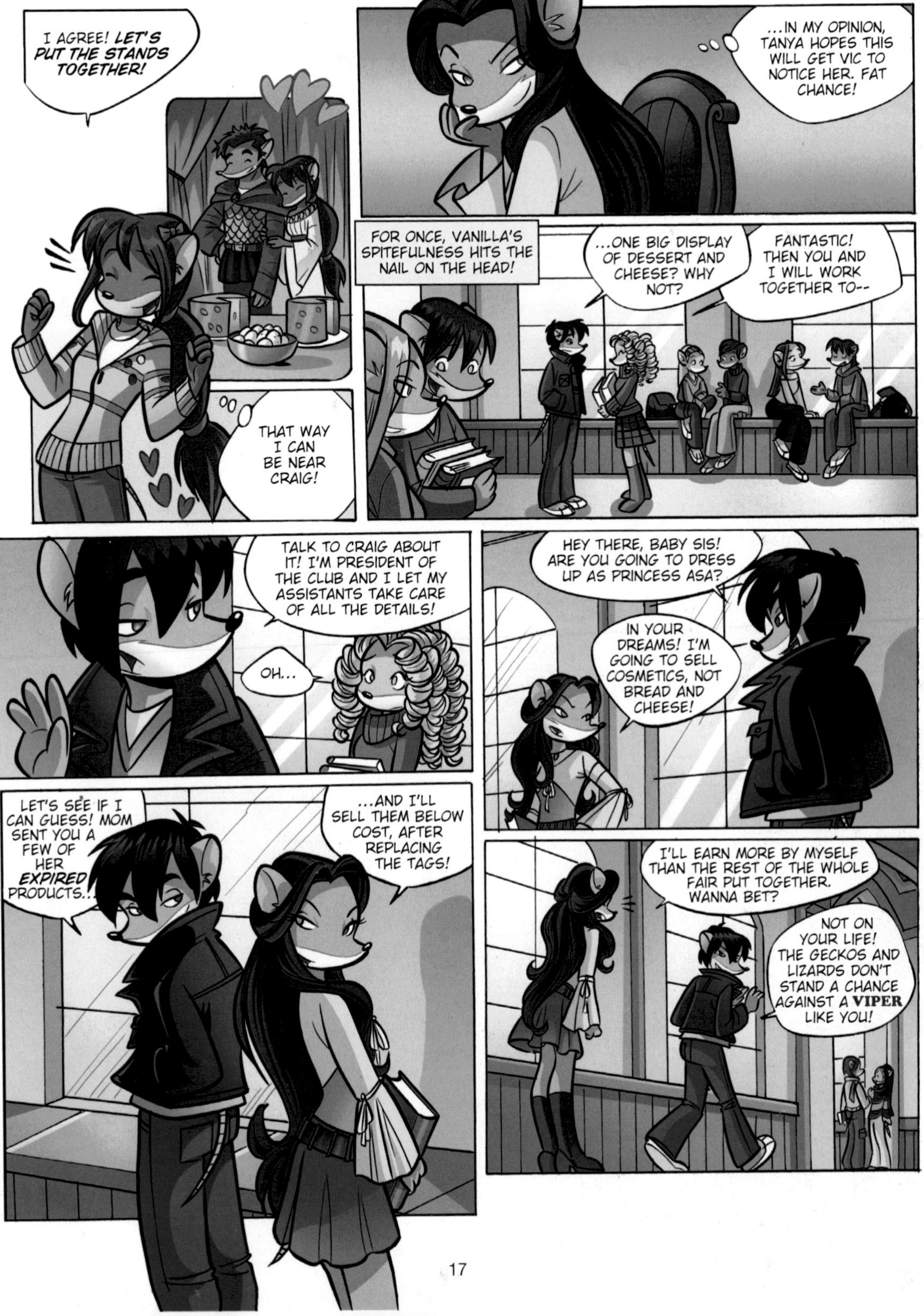
I AGREE! LET'S PUT THE STANDS TOGETHER!
...IN MY OPINION, TANYA HOPES THIS WILL GET VIC TO NOTICE HER. FAT CHANCE!
THAT WAY I CAN BE NEAR CRAIG!
FOR ONCE, VANILLA'S SPITEFULNESS HITS THE NAIL ON THE HEAD!
...ONE BIG DISPLAY OF DESSERT AND CHEESE? WHY NOT?
FANTASTIC! THEN YOU AND I WILL WORK TOGETHER TO--
TALK TO CRAIG ABOUT IT! I'M PRESIDENT OF THE CLUB AND I LET MY ASSISTANTS TAKE CARE OF ALL THE DETAILS!
OH...
HEY THERE, BABY SIS! ARE YOU GOING TO DRESS UP AS PRINCESS ASA?
IN YOUR DREAMS! I'M GOING TO SELL COSMETICS, NOT BREAD AND CHEESE!
LET'S SEE IF I CAN GUESS! MOM SENT YOU A FEW OF HER EXPIRED PRODUCTS...
...AND I'LL SELL THEM BELOW COST, AFTER REPLACING THE TAGS!
I'LL EARN MORE BY MYSELF THAN THE REST OF THE WHOLE FAIR PUT TOGETHER. WANNA BET?
NOT ON YOUR LIFE! THE GECKOS AND LIZARDS DON'T STAND A CHANCE AGAINST A VIPER LIKE YOU!

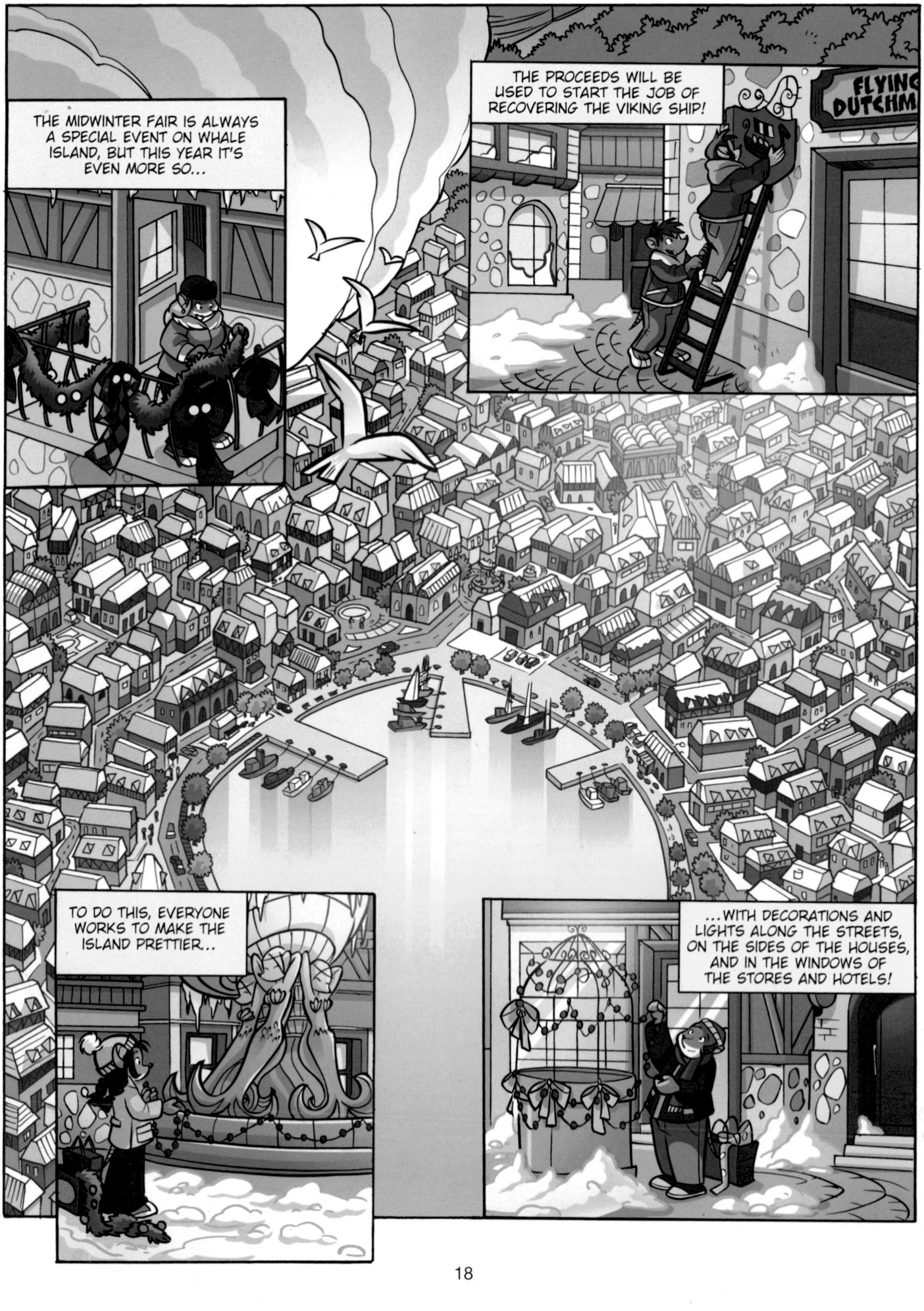
THE MIDWINTER FAIR IS ALWAYS A SPECIAL EVENT ON WHALE ISLAND, BUT THIS YEAR IT'S EVEN MORE SO...
THE PROCEEDS WILL BE USED TO START THE JOB OF RECOVERING THE VIKING SHIP!
FLYING DUTCHM
TO DO THIS, EVERYONE WORKS TO MAKE THE ISLAND PRETTIER...
...WITH DECORATIONS AND LIGHTS ALONG THE STREETS, ON THE SIDES OF THE HOUSES, AND IN THE WINDOWS OF THE STORES AND HOTELS!

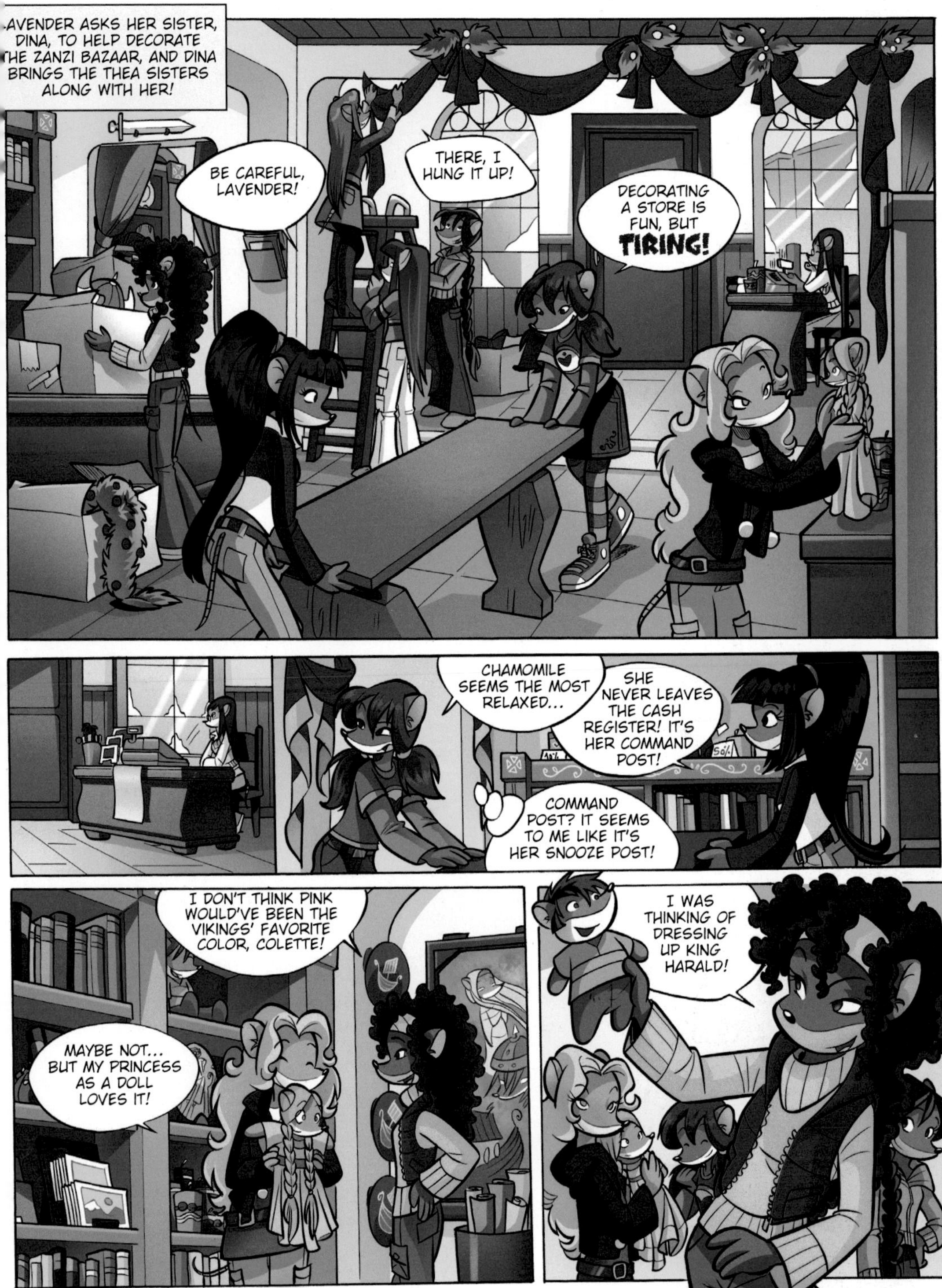
LAVENDER ASKS HER SISTER, DINA, TO HELP DECORATE THE ZANZI BAZAAR, AND DINA BRINGS THE THEA SISTERS ALONG WITH HER!
BE CAREFUL, LAVENDER!
THERE, I HUNG IT UP!
DECORATING A STORE IS FUN, BUT TIRING!
CHAMOMILE SEEMS THE MOST RELAXED...
SHE NEVER LEAVES THE CASH REGISTER! IT'S HER COMMAND POST!
COMMAND POST? IT SEEMS TO ME LIKE IT'S HER SNOOZE POST!
I DON'T THINK PINK WOULD'VE BEEN THE VIKINGS' FAVORITE COLOR, COLETTE!
MAYBE NOT... BUT MY PRINCESS AS A DOLL LOVES IT!
I WAS THINKING OF DRESSING UP KING HARALD!

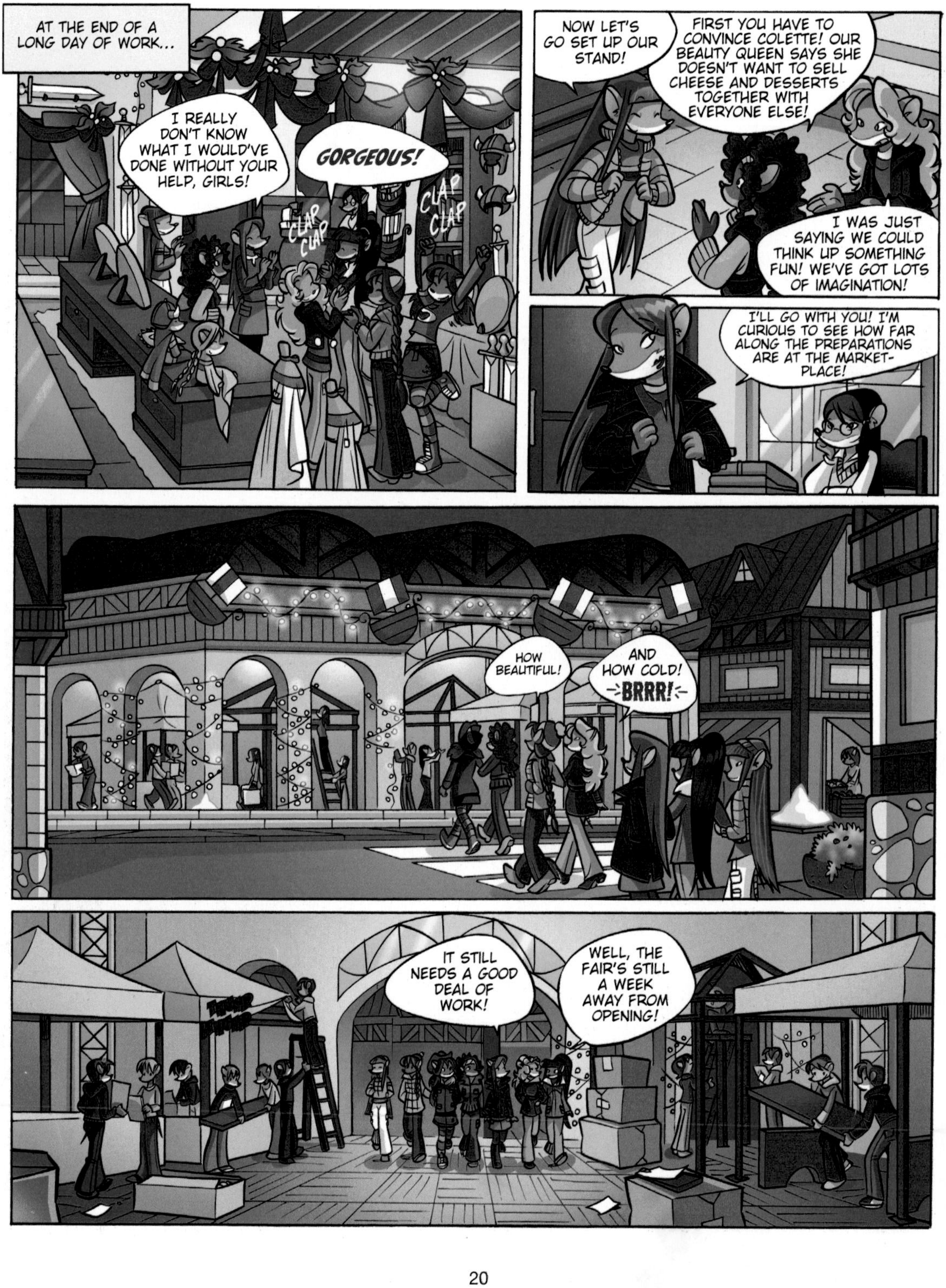
AT THE END OF A LONG DAY OF WORK...
I REALLY DON'T KNOW WHAT I WOULD'VE DONE WITHOUT YOUR HELP, GIRLS!
GORGEOUS!
CLAP CLAP
CLAP CLAP
NOW LET'S GO SET UP OUR STAND!
FIRST YOU HAVE TO CONVINCE COLETTE! OUR BEAUTY QUEEN SAYS SHE DOESN'T WANT TO SELL CHEESE AND DESSERTS TOGETHER WITH EVERYONE ELSE!
I WAS JUST SAYING WE COULD THINK UP SOMETHING FUN! WE'VE GOT LOTS OF IMAGINATION!
I'LL GO WITH YOU! I'M CURIOUS TO SEE HOW FAR ALONG THE PREPARATIONS ARE AT THE MARKET-PLACE!
HOW BEAUTIFUL!
AND HOW COLD! BRRR!
IT STILL NEEDS A GOOD DEAL OF WORK!
WELL, THE FAIR'S STILL A WEEK AWAY FROM OPENING!

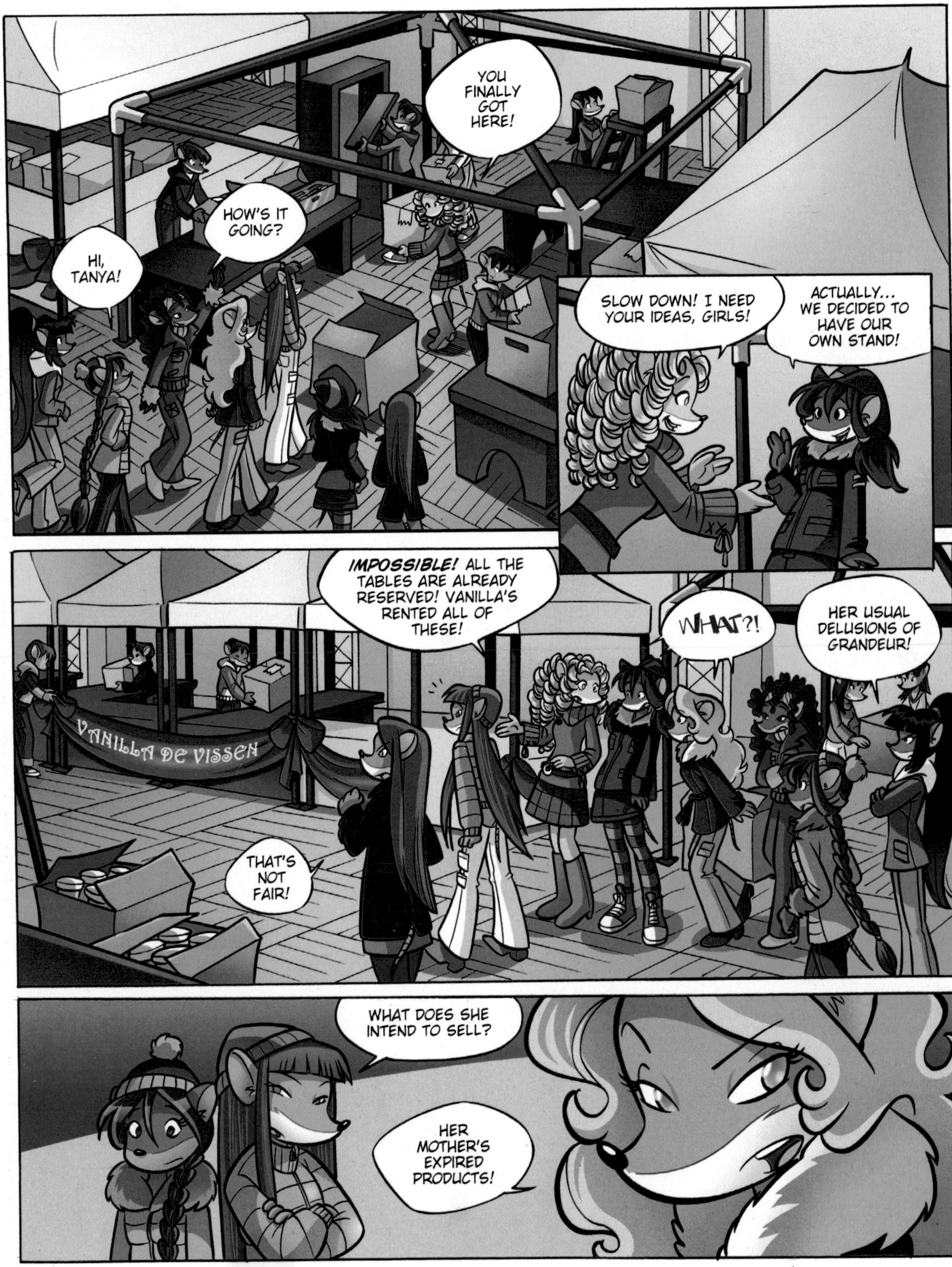
YOU FINALLY GOT HERE!
HI, TANYA!
HOW'S IT GOING?
SLOW DOWN! I NEED YOUR IDEAS, GIRLS!
ACTUALLY... WE DECIDED TO HAVE OUR OWN STAND!
IMPOSSIBLE! ALL THE TABLES ARE ALREADY RESERVED! VANILLA'S RENTED ALL OF THESE!
WHAT?!
HER USUAL DELUSIONS OF GRANDEUR!
VANILLA DE VISSEN
THAT'S NOT FAIR!
WHAT DOES SHE INTEND TO SELL?
HER MOTHER'S EXPIRED PRODUCTS!

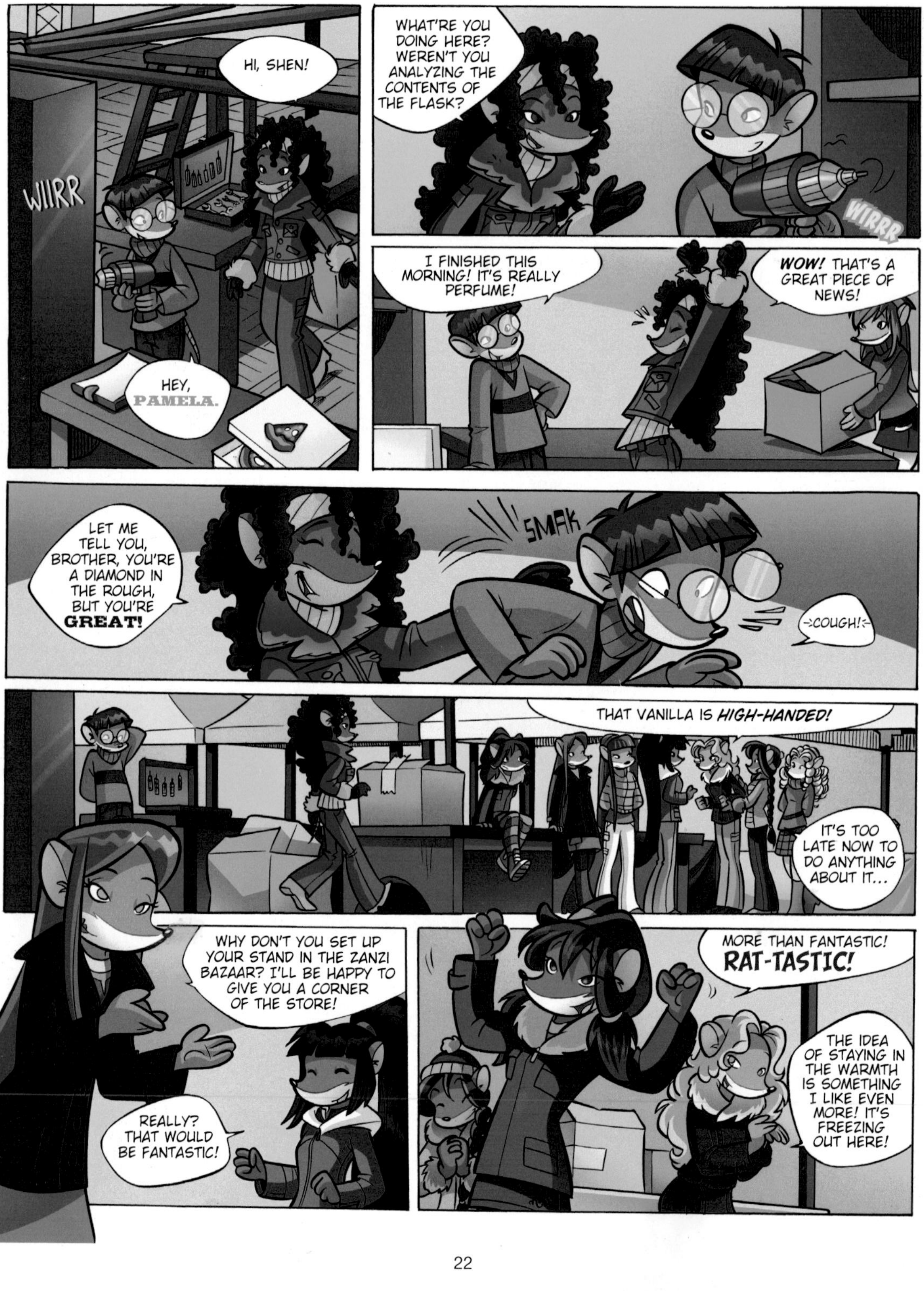
HI, SHEN!
WIIRR
HEY, PAMELA.
WHAT'RE YOU DOING HERE? WEREN'T YOU ANALYZING THE CONTENTS OF THE FLASK?
WIRRR
I FINISHED THIS MORNING! IT'S REALLY PERFUME!
WOW! THAT'S A GREAT PIECE OF NEWS!
LET ME TELL YOU, BROTHER, YOU'RE A DIAMOND IN THE ROUGH, BUT YOU'RE GREAT!
SMAK
COUGH!
THAT VANILLA IS HIGH-HANDED!
IT'S TOO LATE NOW TO DO ANYTHING ABOUT IT...
WHY DON'T YOU SET UP YOUR STAND IN THE ZANZI BAZAAR? I'LL BE HAPPY TO GIVE YOU A CORNER OF THE STORE!
REALLY? THAT WOULD BE FANTASTIC!
MORE THAN FANTASTIC! RAT-TASTIC!
THE IDEA OF STAYING IN THE WARMTH IS SOMETHING I LIKE EVEN MORE! IT'S FREEZING OUT HERE!

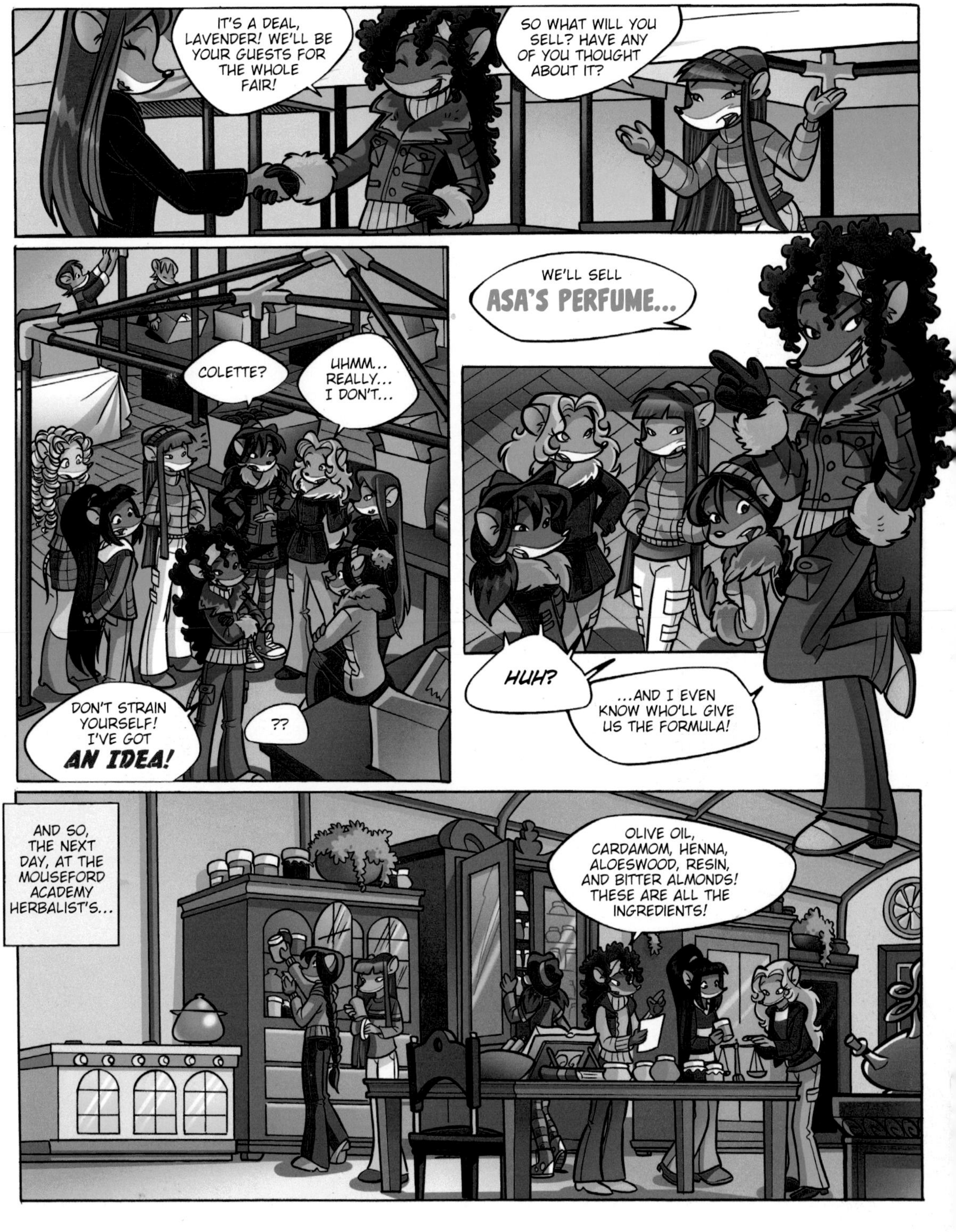
IT'S A DEAL, LAVENDER! WE'LL BE YOUR GUESTS FOR THE WHOLE FAIR!
SO WHAT WILL YOU SELL? HAVE ANY OF YOU THOUGHT ABOUT IT?
COLETTE?
UHMM... REALLY... I DON'T...
DON'T STRAIN YOURSELF! I'VE GOT AN IDEA!
??
WE'LL SELL ASA'S PERFUME...
HUH?
...AND I EVEN KNOW WHO'LL GIVE US THE FORMULA!
AND SO, THE NEXT DAY, AT THE MOUSEFORD ACADEMY HERBALIST'S...
OLIVE OIL, CARDAMOM, HENNA, ALOESWOOD, RESIN, AND BITTER ALMONDS! THESE ARE ALL THE INGREDIENTS!

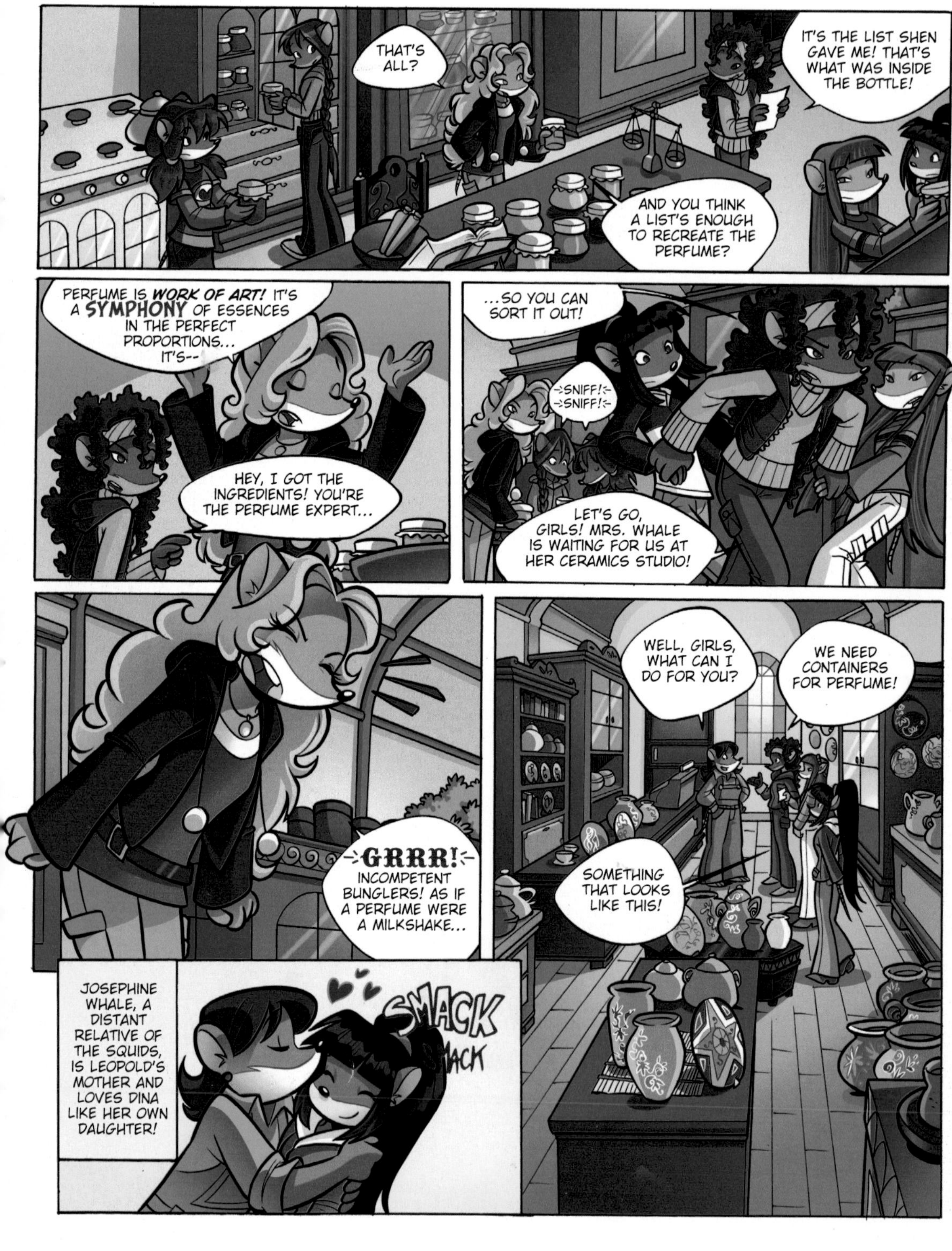
THAT'S ALL?
IT'S THE LIST SHEN GAVE ME! THAT'S WHAT WAS INSIDE THE BOTTLE!
AND YOU THINK A LIST'S ENOUGH TO RECREATE THE PERFUME?
PERFUME IS WORK OF ART! IT'S A SYMPHONY OF ESSENCES IN THE PERFECT PROPORTIONS... IT'S--
HEY, I GOT THE INGREDIENTS! YOU'RE THE PERFUME EXPERT...
...SO YOU CAN SORT IT OUT!
SNIFF! SNIFF!
LET'S GO, GIRLS! MRS. WHALE IS WAITING FOR US AT HER CERAMICS STUDIO!
GRRRR! INCOMPETENT BUNGLERS! AS IF A PERFUME WERE A MILKSHAKE...
WELL, GIRLS, WHAT CAN I DO FOR YOU?
WE NEED CONTAINERS FOR PERFUME!
SOMETHING THAT LOOKS LIKE THIS!
JOSEPHINE WHALE, A DISTANT RELATIVE OF THE SQUIDS, IS LEOPOLD'S MOTHER AND LOVES DINA LIKE HER OWN DAUGHTER!
SMACK
SMACK

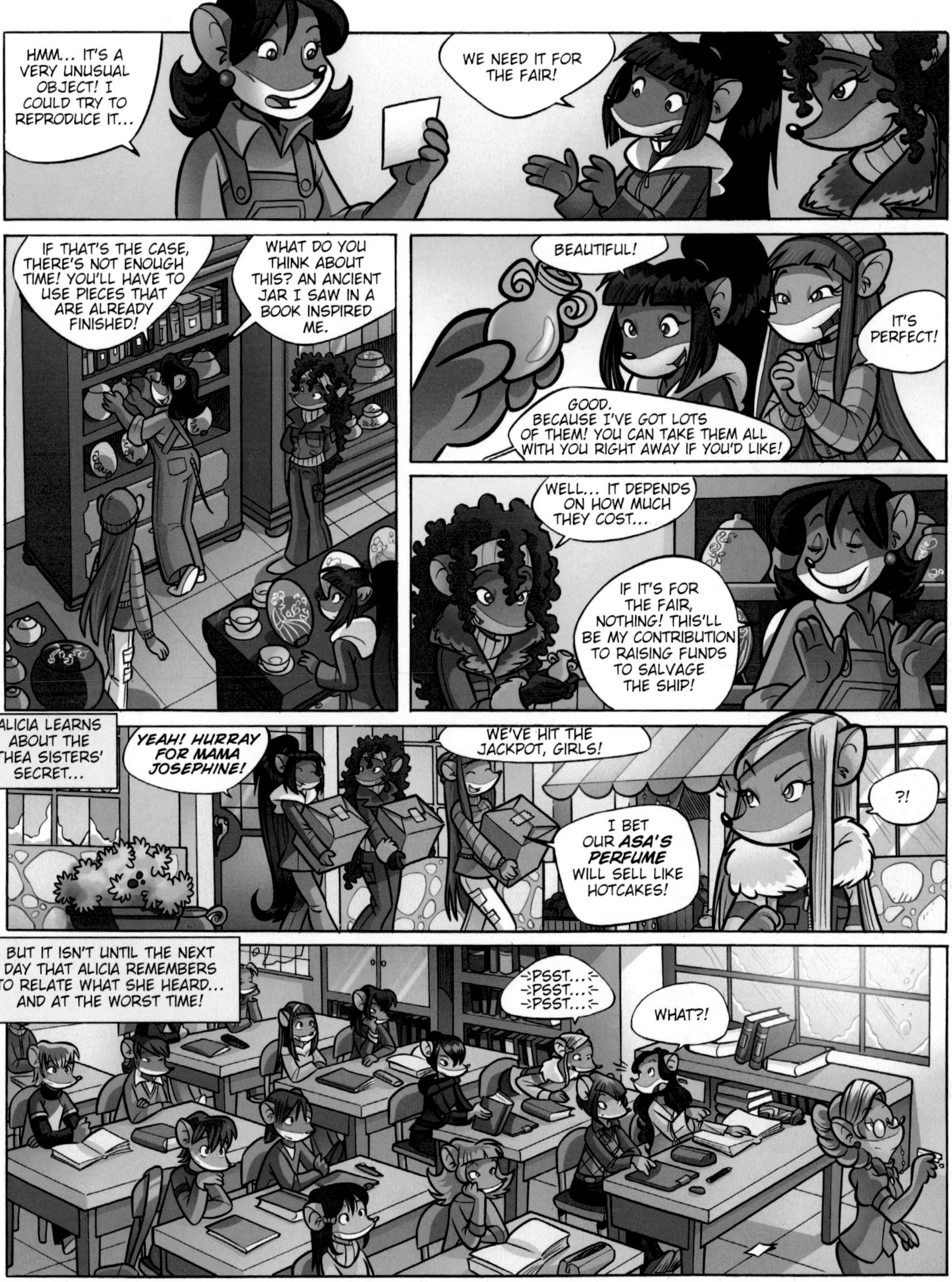
HMM... IT'S A VERY UNUSUAL OBJECT! I COULD TRY TO REPRODUCE IT...
WE NEED IT FOR THE FAIR!
IF THAT'S THE CASE, THERE'S NOT ENOUGH TIME! YOU'LL HAVE TO USE PIECES THAT ARE ALREADY FINISHED!
WHAT DO YOU THINK ABOUT THIS? AN ANCIENT JAR I SAW IN A BOOK INSPIRED ME.
BEAUTIFUL!
IT'S PERFECT!
GOOD. BECAUSE I'VE GOT LOTS OF THEM! YOU CAN TAKE THEM ALL WITH YOU RIGHT AWAY IF YOU'D LIKE!
WELL... IT DEPENDS ON HOW MUCH THEY COST...
IF IT'S FOR THE FAIR, NOTHING! THIS'LL BE MY CONTRIBUTION TO RAISING FUNDS TO SALVAGE THE SHIP!
ALICIA LEARNS ABOUT THE THEA SISTERS' SECRET...
YEAH! HURRAY FOR MAMA JOSEPHINE!
WE'VE HIT THE JACKPOT, GIRLS!
I BET OUR ASA'S PERFUME WILL SELL LIKE HOTCAKES!
?!
BUT IT ISN'T UNTIL THE NEXT DAY THAT ALICIA REMEMBERS TO RELATE WHAT SHE HEARD... AND AT THE WORST TIME!
PSST... PSST... PSST...
WHAT?!

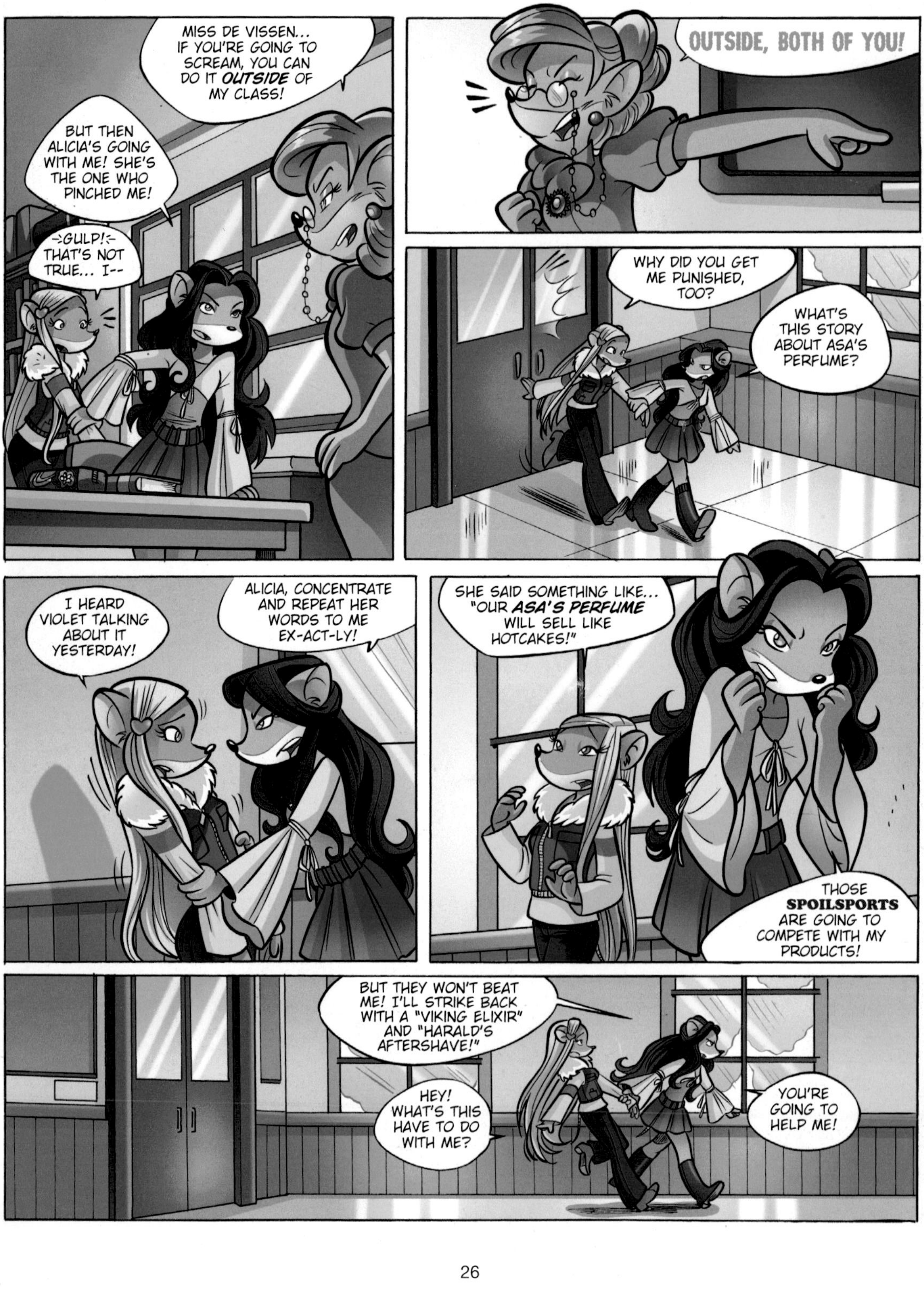
MISS DE VISSEN... IF YOU'RE GOING TO SCREAM, YOU CAN DO IT OUTSIDE OF MY CLASS!
BUT THEN ALICIA'S GOING WITH ME! SHE'S THE ONE WHO PINCHED ME!
GULP! THAT'S NOT TRUE... I--
OUTSIDE, BOTH OF YOU!
WHY DID YOU GET ME PUNISHED, TOO?
WHAT'S THIS STORY ABOUT ASA'S PERFUME?
I HEARD VIOLET TALKING ABOUT IT YESTERDAY!
ALICIA, CONCENTRATE AND REPEAT HER WORDS TO ME EX-ACT-LY!
SHE SAID SOMETHING LIKE... "OUR ASA'S PERFUME WILL SELL LIKE HOTCAKES!"
THOSE SPOILSPORTS ARE GOING TO COMPETE WITH MY PRODUCTS!
BUT THEY WON'T BEAT ME! I'LL STRIKE BACK WITH A "VIKING ELIXIR" AND "HARALD'S AFTERSHAVE!"
HEY! WHAT'S THIS HAVE TO DO WITH ME?
YOU'RE GOING TO HELP ME!

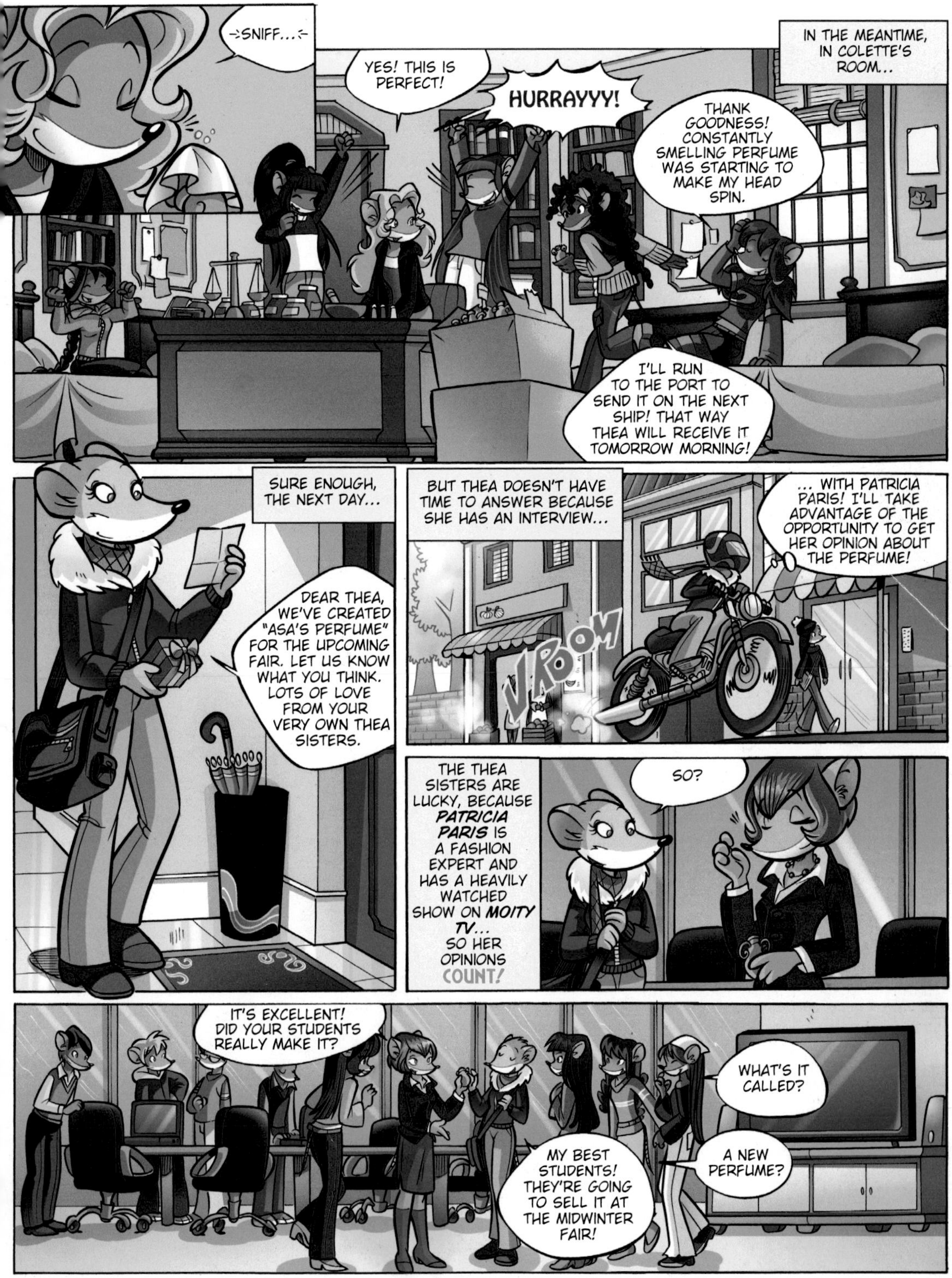
-SNIFF...-
IN THE MEANTIME, IN COLETTE'S ROOM...
YES! THIS IS PERFECT!
HURRAYYY!
THANK GOODNESS! CONSTANTLY SMELLING PERFUME WAS STARTING TO MAKE MY HEAD SPIN.
I'LL RUN TO THE PORT TO SEND IT ON THE NEXT SHIP! THAT WAY THEA WILL RECEIVE IT TOMORROW MORNING!
SURE ENOUGH, THE NEXT DAY...
DEAR THEA, WE'VE CREATED "ASA'S PERFUME" FOR THE UPCOMING FAIR. LET US KNOW WHAT YOU THINK. LOTS OF LOVE FROM YOUR VERY OWN THEA SISTERS.
BUT THEA DOESN'T HAVE TIME TO ANSWER BECAUSE SHE HAS AN INTERVIEW...
... WITH PATRICIA PARIS! I'LL TAKE ADVANTAGE OF THE OPPORTUNITY TO GET HER OPINION ABOUT THE PERFUME!
VROOM
THE THEA SISTERS ARE LUCKY, BECAUSE PATRICIA PARIS IS A FASHION EXPERT AND HAS A HEAVILY WATCHED SHOW ON MOITY TV... SO HER OPINIONS COUNT!
SO?
IT'S EXCELLENT! DID YOUR STUDENTS REALLY MAKE IT?
MY BEST STUDENTS! THEY'RE GOING TO SELL IT AT THE MIDWINTER FAIR!
WHAT'S IT CALLED?
A NEW PERFUME?

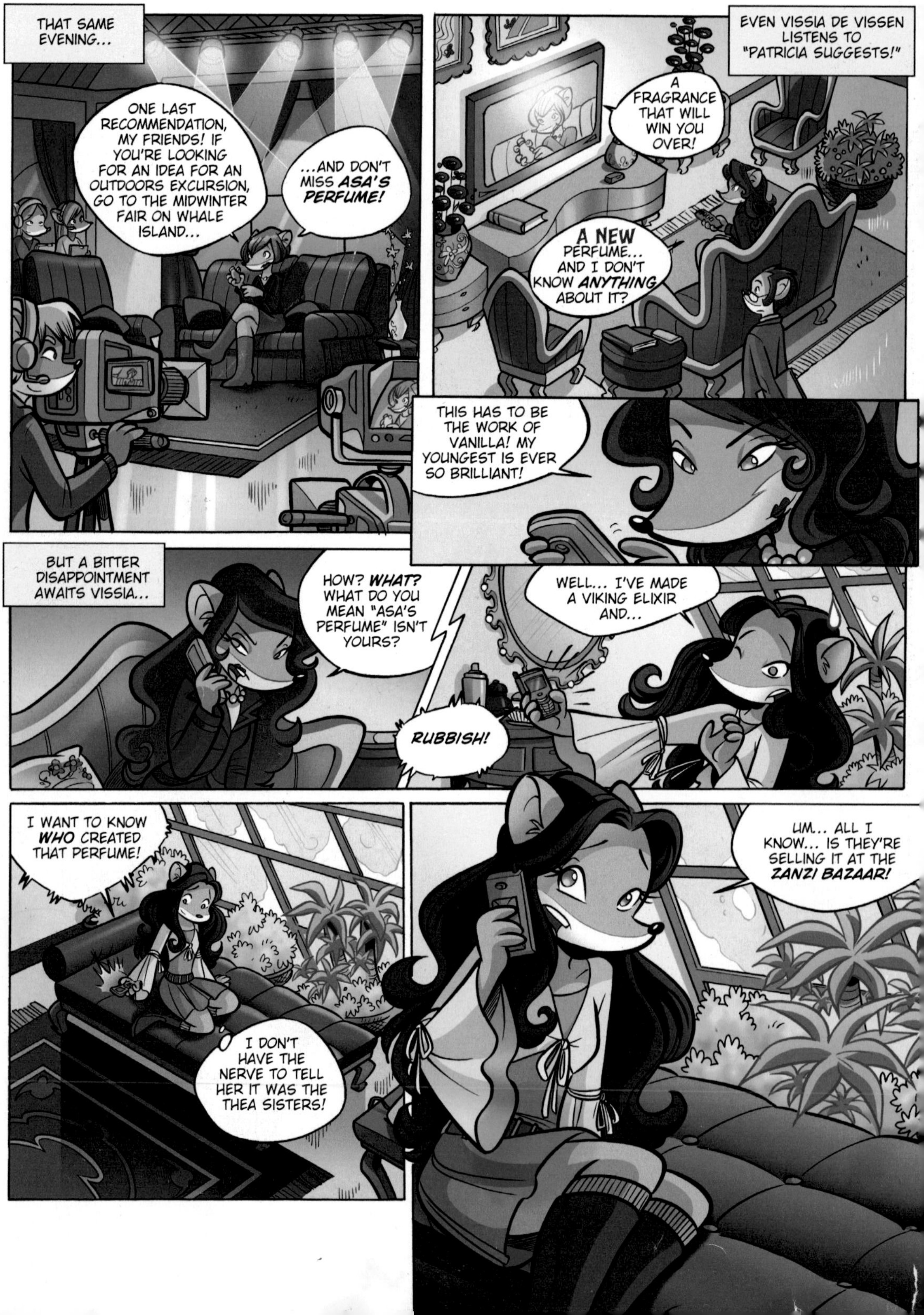
THAT SAME EVENING...
ONE LAST RECOMMENDATION, MY FRIENDS! IF YOU'RE LOOKING FOR AN IDEA FOR AN OUTDOORS EXCURSION, GO TO THE MIDWINTER FAIR ON WHALE ISLAND...
...AND DON'T MISS ASA'S PERFUME!
EVEN VISSIA DE VISSEN LISTENS TO "PATRICIA SUGGESTS!"
A FRAGRANCE THAT WILL WIN YOU OVER!
A NEW PERFUME... AND I DON'T KNOW ANYTHING ABOUT IT?
THIS HAS TO BE THE WORK OF VANILLA! MY YOUNGEST IS EVER SO BRILLIANT!
BUT A BITTER DISAPPOINTMENT AWAITS VISSIA...
HOW? WHAT? WHAT DO YOU MEAN "ASA'S PERFUME" ISN'T YOURS?
WELL... I'VE MADE A VIKING ELIXIR AND...
RUBBISH!
I WANT TO KNOW WHO CREATED THAT PERFUME!
I DON'T HAVE THE NERVE TO TELL HER IT WAS THE THEA SISTERS!
UM... ALL I KNOW... IS THEY'RE SELLING IT AT THE ZANZI BAZAAR!

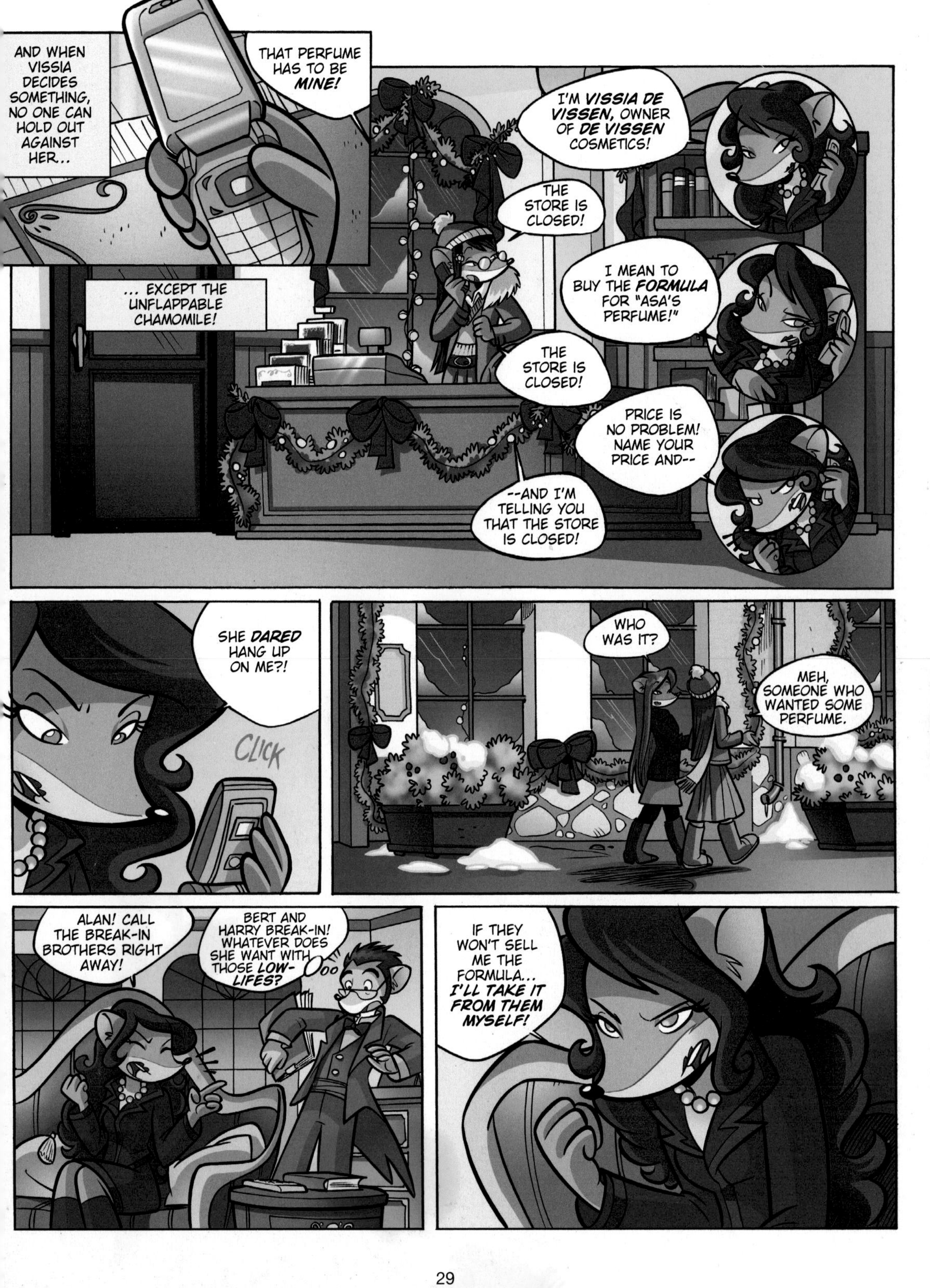
AND WHEN VISSIA DECIDES SOMETHING, NO ONE CAN HOLD OUT AGAINST HER...
THAT PERFUME HAS TO BE *MINE!*
I'M *VISSIA DE VISSEN,* OWNER OF *DE VISSEN* COSMETICS!
THE STORE IS CLOSED!
... EXCEPT THE UNFLAPPABLE CHAMOMILE!
I MEAN TO BUY THE *FORMULA* FOR "ASA'S PERFUME!"
THE STORE IS CLOSED!
PRICE IS NO PROBLEM! NAME YOUR PRICE AND--
--AND I'M TELLING YOU THAT THE STORE IS CLOSED!
SHE *DARED* HANG UP ON ME?!
CLICK
WHO WAS IT?
MEH, SOMEONE WHO WANTED SOME PERFUME.
ALAN! CALL THE BREAK-IN BROTHERS RIGHT AWAY!
BERT AND HARRY BREAK-IN! WHATEVER DOES SHE WANT WITH THOSE *LOW-LIFES?*
IF THEY WON'T SELL ME THE FORMULA... *I'LL TAKE IT FROM THEM MYSELF!*

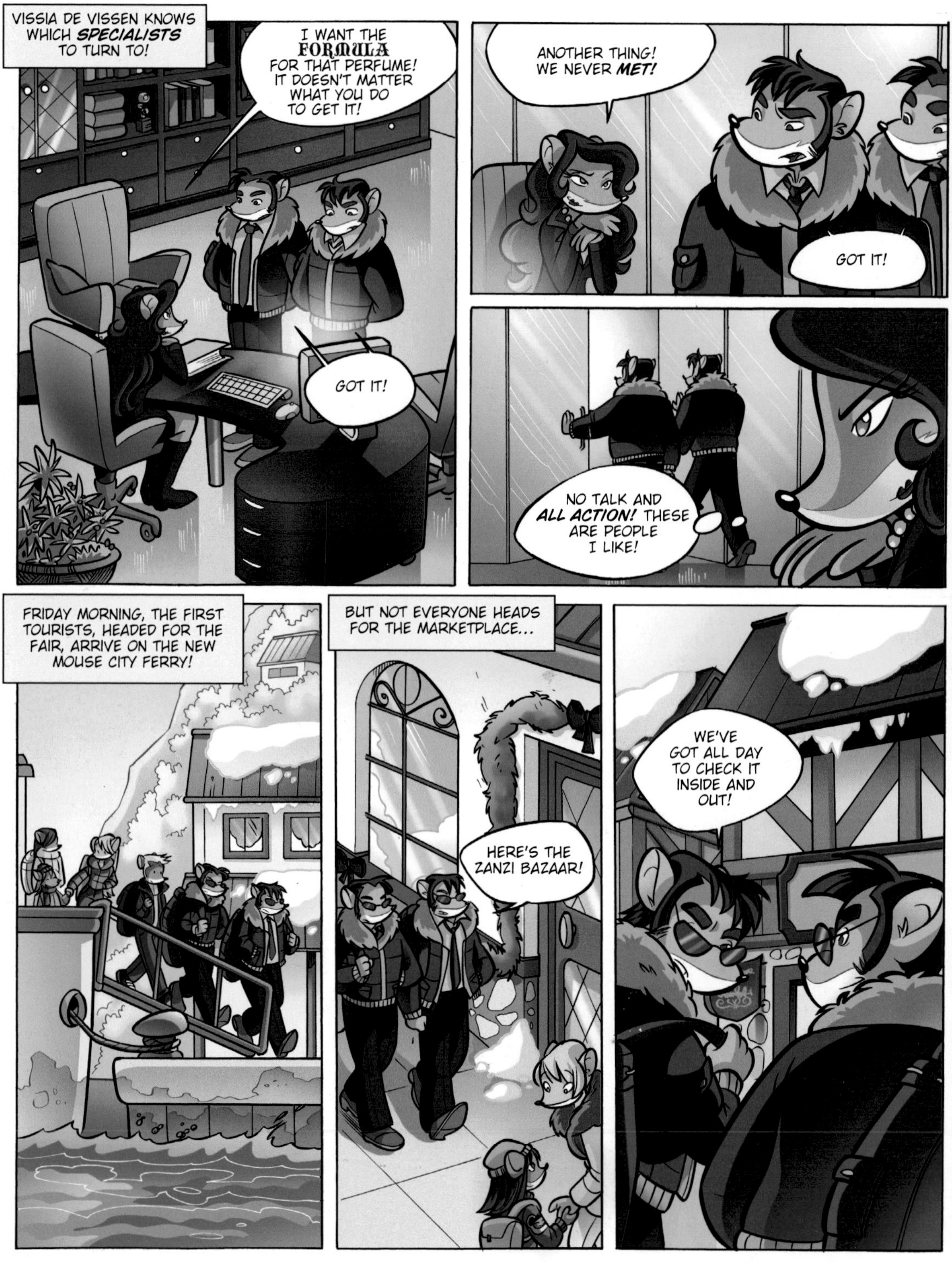
VISSIA DE VISSEN KNOWS WHICH SPECIALISTS TO TURN TO!
I WANT THE FORMULA FOR THAT PERFUME! IT DOESN'T MATTER WHAT YOU DO TO GET IT!
GOT IT!
ANOTHER THING! WE NEVER MET!
GOT IT!
NO TALK AND ALL ACTION! THESE ARE PEOPLE I LIKE!
FRIDAY MORNING, THE FIRST TOURISTS, HEADED FOR THE FAIR, ARRIVE ON THE NEW MOUSE CITY FERRY!
BUT NOT EVERYONE HEADS FOR THE MARKETPLACE...
HERE'S THE ZANZI BAZAAR!
WE'VE GOT ALL DAY TO CHECK IT INSIDE AND OUT!

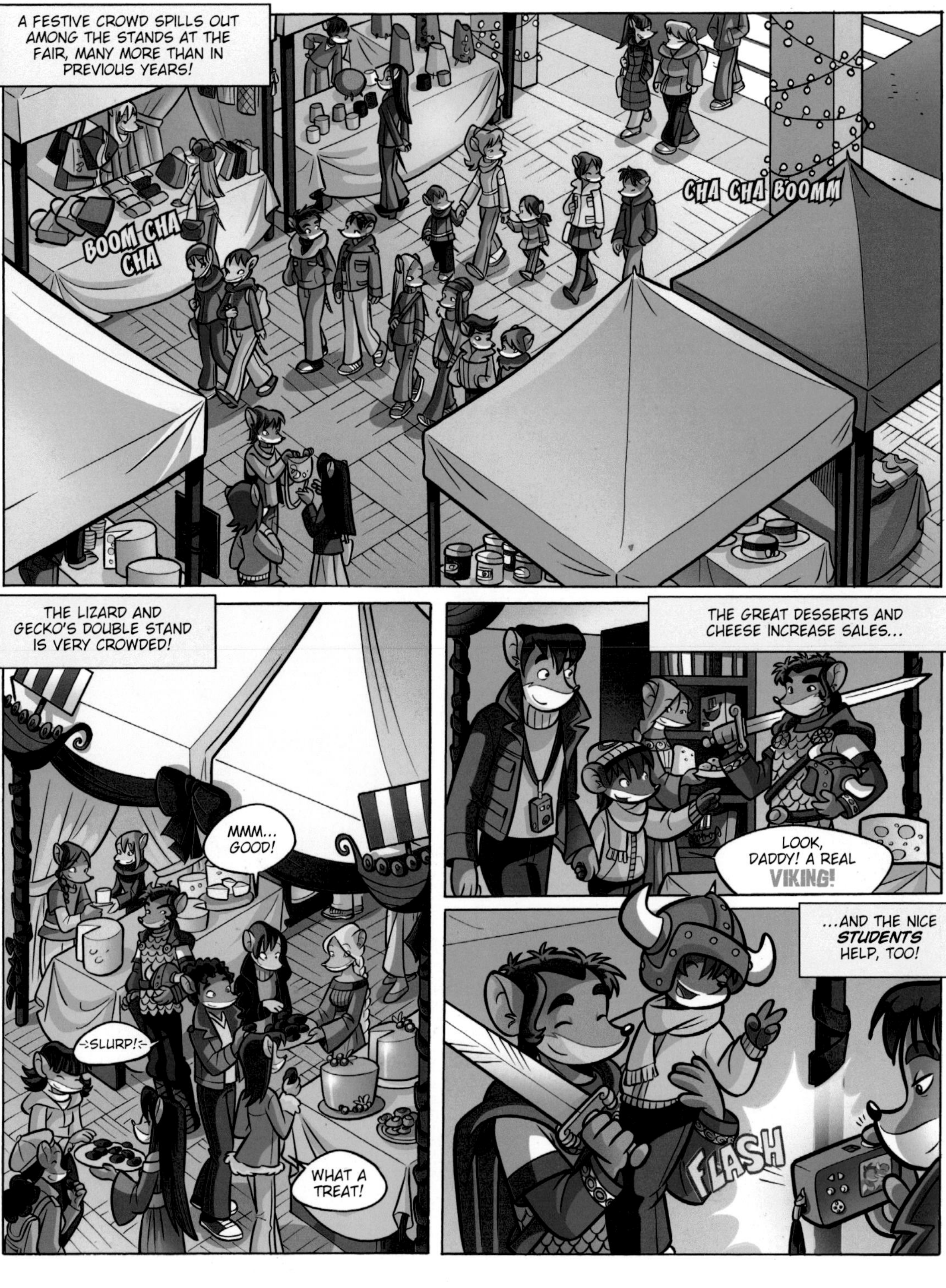
A FESTIVE CROWD SPILLS OUT AMONG THE STANDS AT THE FAIR, MANY MORE THAN IN PREVIOUS YEARS!
BOOM CHA CHA
CHA CHA BOOMM
THE LIZARD AND GECKO'S DOUBLE STAND IS VERY CROWDED!
MMM... GOOD!
-SLURP!-
WHAT A TREAT!
THE GREAT DESSERTS AND CHEESE INCREASE SALES...
LOOK, DADDY! A REAL VIKING!
...AND THE NICE STUDENTS HELP, TOO!
FLASH

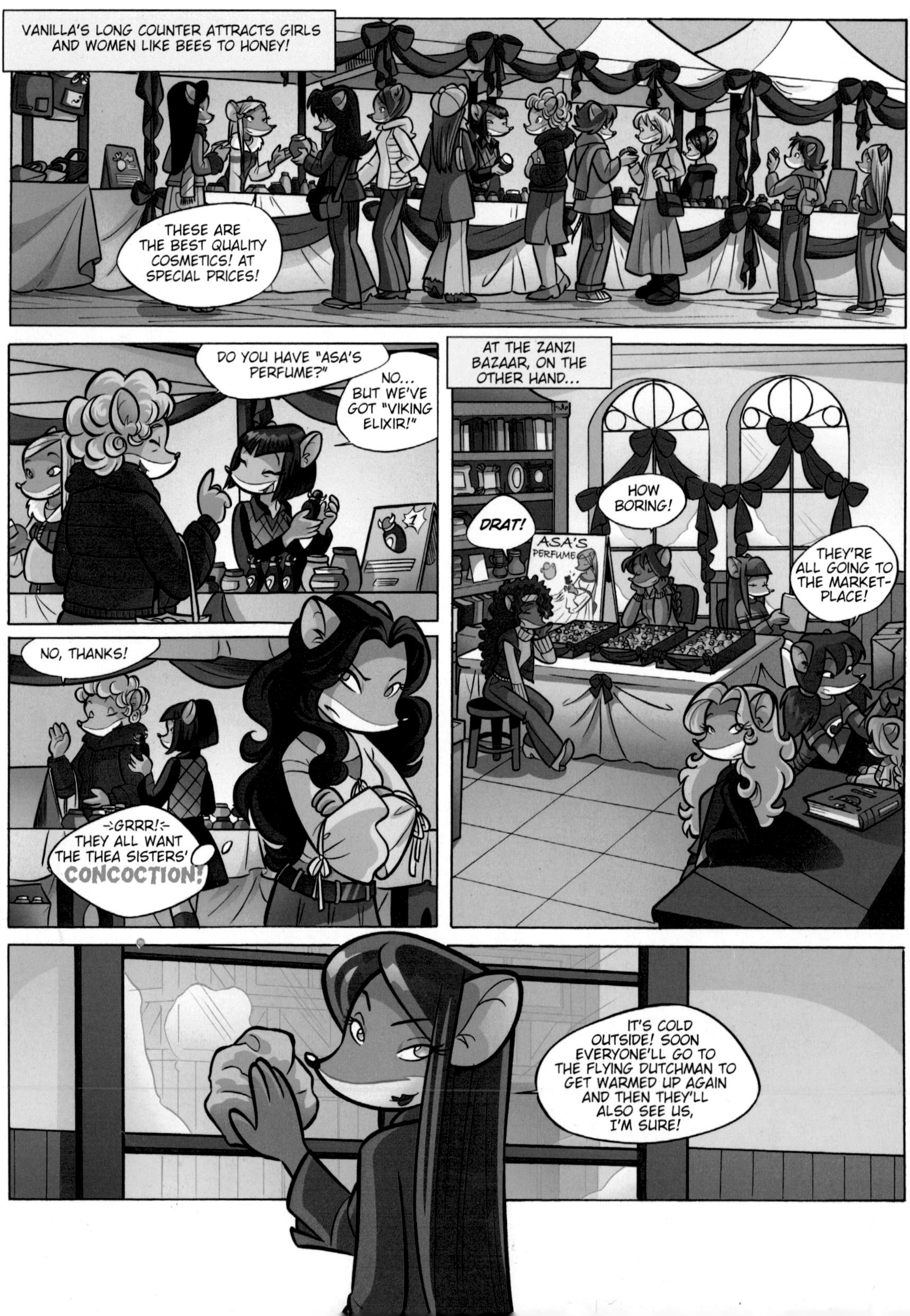
VANILLA'S LONG COUNTER ATTRACTS GIRLS AND WOMEN LIKE BEES TO HONEY!
THESE ARE THE BEST QUALITY COSMETICS! AT SPECIAL PRICES!
DO YOU HAVE "ASA'S PERFUME?"
NO... BUT WE'VE GOT "VIKING ELIXIR!"
NO, THANKS!
GRRR! THEY ALL WANT THE THEA SISTERS' CONCOCTION!
AT THE ZANZI BAZAAR, ON THE OTHER HAND...
DRAT!
HOW BORING!
ASA'S PERFUME
THEY'RE ALL GOING TO THE MARKET-PLACE!
IT'S COLD OUTSIDE! SOON EVERYONE'LL GO TO THE FLYING DUTCHMAN TO GET WARMED UP AGAIN AND THEN THEY'LL ALSO SEE US, I'M SURE!

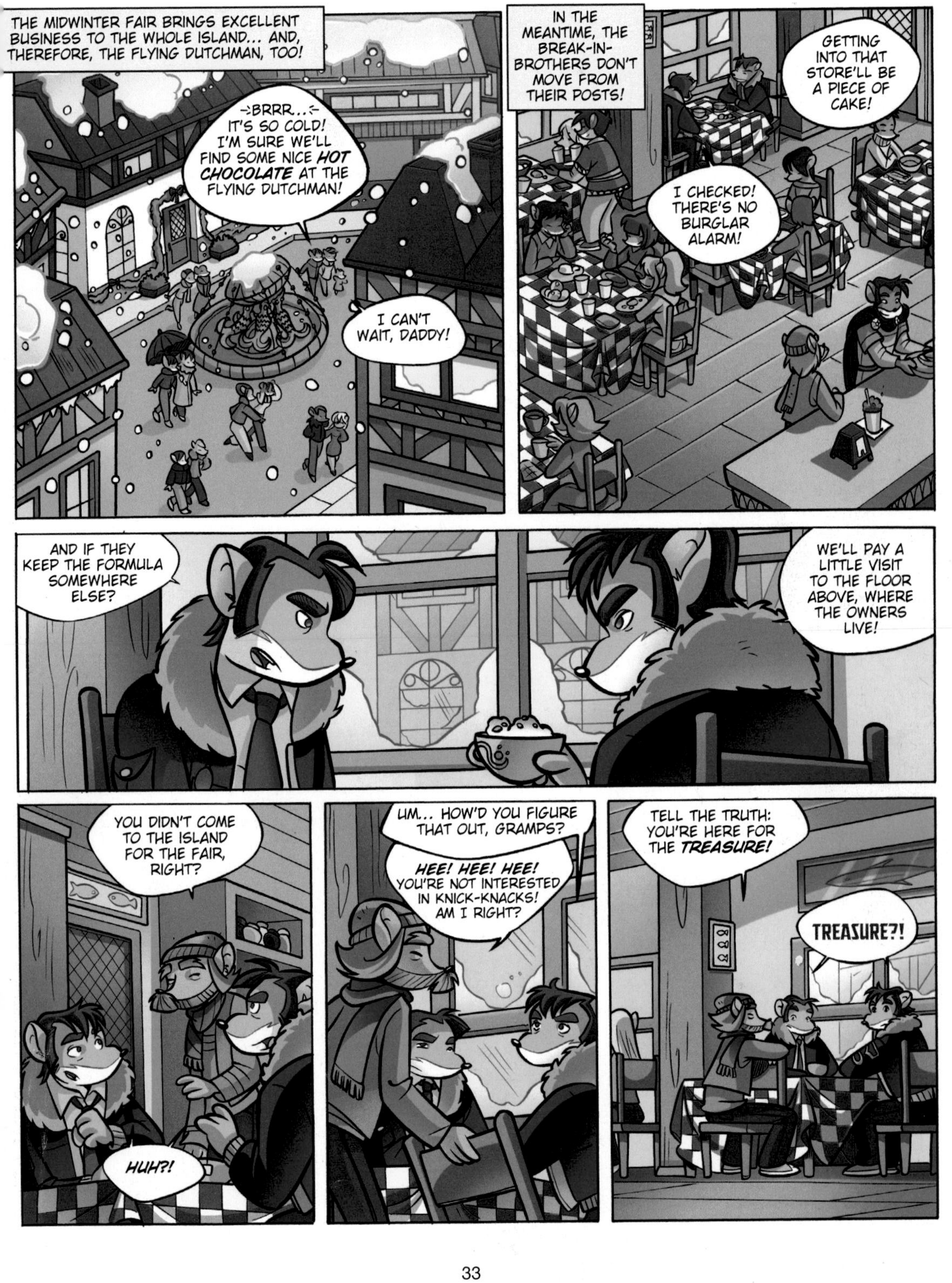

THE MIDWINTER FAIR BRINGS EXCELLENT BUSINESS TO THE WHOLE ISLAND... AND, THEREFORE, THE FLYING DUTCHMAN, TOO!
BRRR... IT'S SO COLD! I'M SURE WE'LL FIND SOME NICE HOT CHOCOLATE AT THE FLYING DUTCHMAN!
I CAN'T WAIT, DADDY!
IN THE MEANTIME, THE BREAK-IN-BROTHERS DON'T MOVE FROM THEIR POSTS!
GETTING INTO THAT STORE'LL BE A PIECE OF CAKE!
I CHECKED! THERE'S NO BURGLAR ALARM!
AND IF THEY KEEP THE FORMULA SOMEWHERE ELSE?
WE'LL PAY A LITTLE VISIT TO THE FLOOR ABOVE, WHERE THE OWNERS LIVE!
YOU DIDN'T COME TO THE ISLAND FOR THE FAIR, RIGHT?
HUH?!
UM... HOW'D YOU FIGURE THAT OUT, GRAMPS?
HEE! HEE! HEE! YOU'RE NOT INTERESTED IN KNICK-KNACKS! AM I RIGHT?
TELL THE TRUTH: YOU'RE HERE FOR THE TREASURE!
TREASURE?!

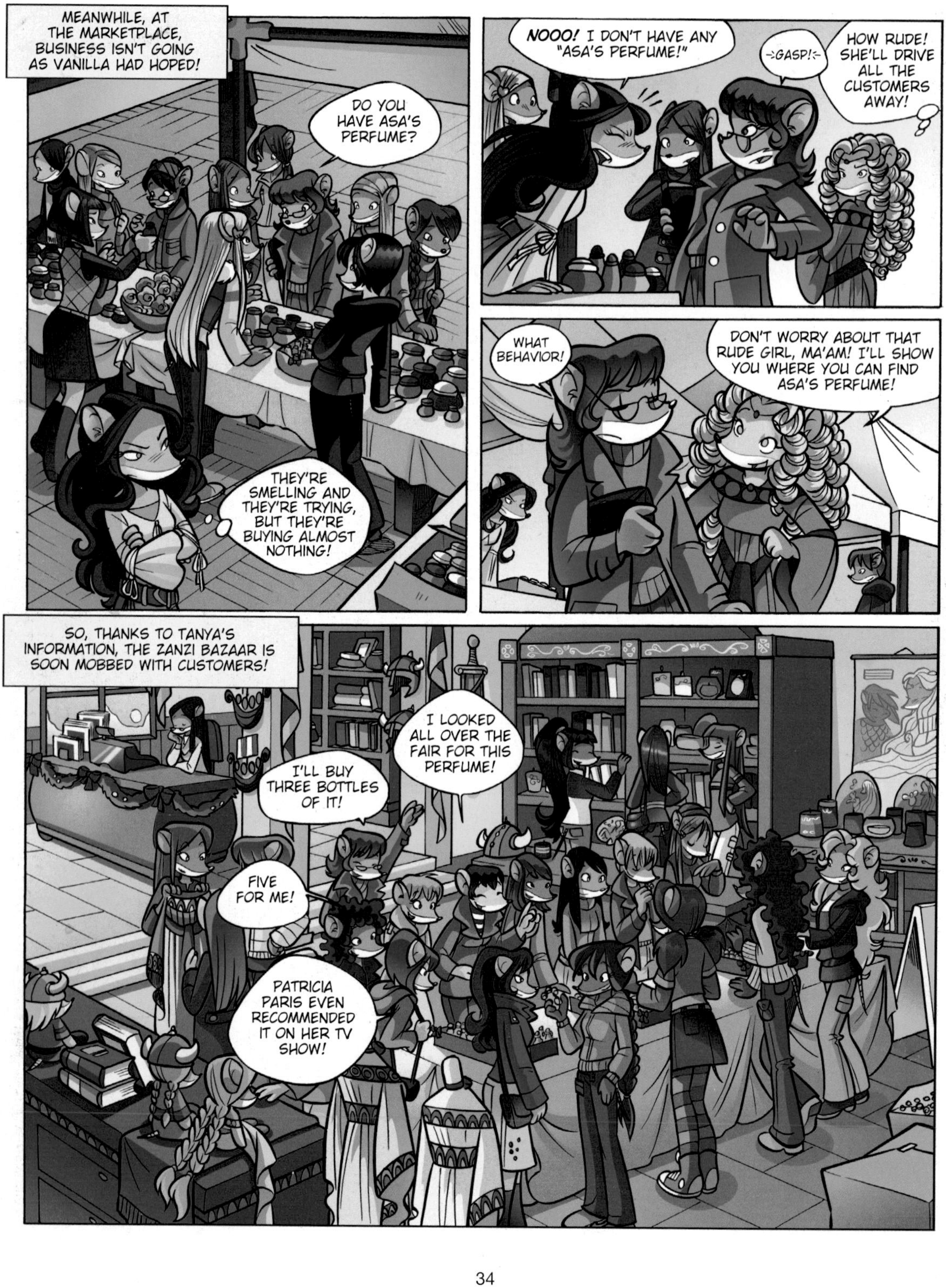
MEANWHILE, AT THE MARKETPLACE, BUSINESS ISN'T GOING AS VANILLA HAD HOPED!
DO YOU HAVE ASA'S PERFUME?
THEY'RE SMELLING AND THEY'RE TRYING, BUT THEY'RE BUYING ALMOST NOTHING!
NOOO! I DON'T HAVE ANY "ASA'S PERFUME!"
GASP!
HOW RUDE! SHE'LL DRIVE ALL THE CUSTOMERS AWAY!
WHAT BEHAVIOR!
DON'T WORRY ABOUT THAT RUDE GIRL, MA'AM! I'LL SHOW YOU WHERE YOU CAN FIND ASA'S PERFUME!
SO, THANKS TO TANYA'S INFORMATION, THE ZANZI BAZAAR IS SOON MOBBED WITH CUSTOMERS!
I LOOKED ALL OVER THE FAIR FOR THIS PERFUME!
I'LL BUY THREE BOTTLES OF IT!
FIVE FOR ME!
PATRICIA PARIS EVEN RECOMMENDED IT ON HER TV SHOW!

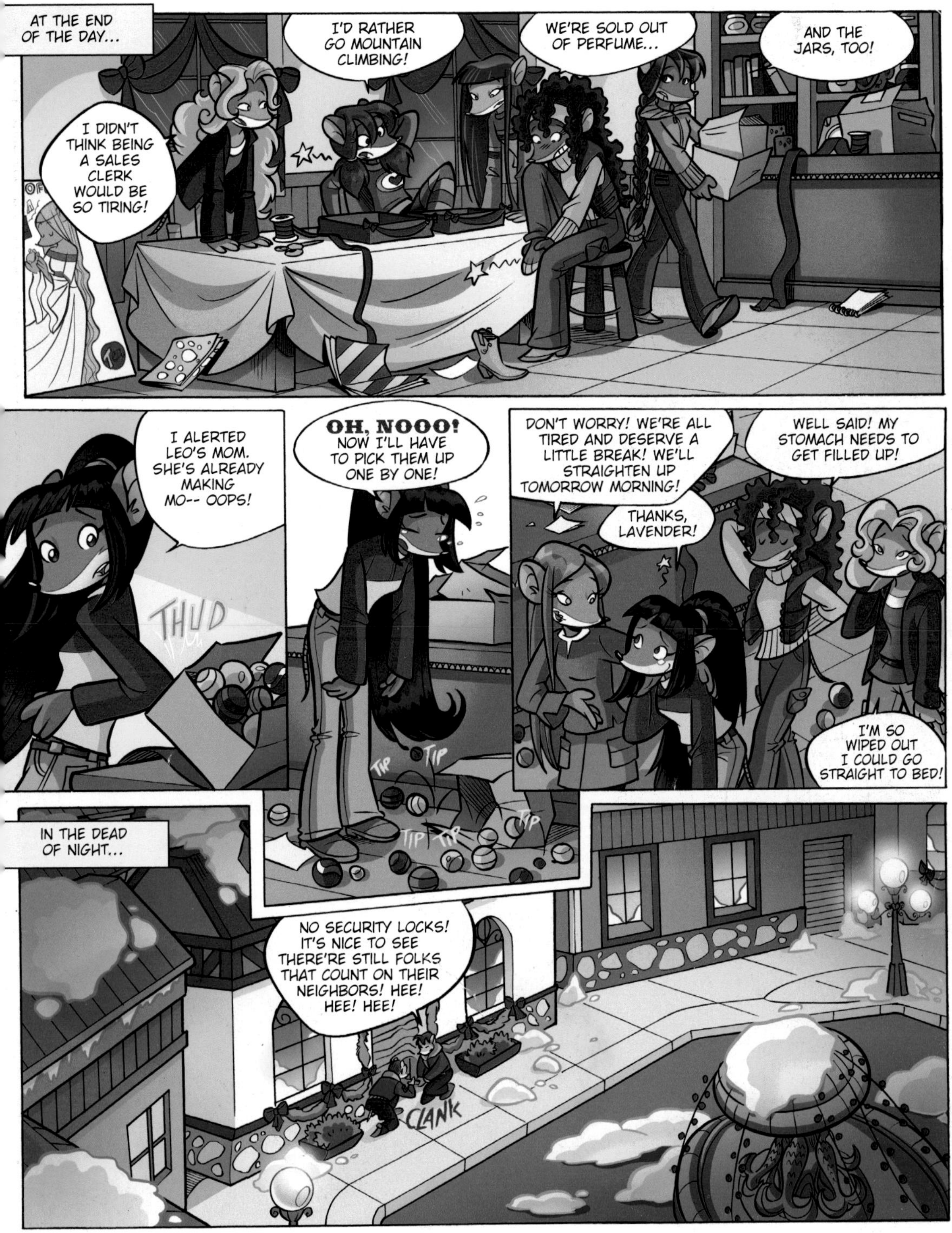
AT THE END OF THE DAY...
I DIDN'T THINK BEING A SALES CLERK WOULD BE SO TIRING!
I'D RATHER GO MOUNTAIN CLIMBING!
WE'RE SOLD OUT OF PERFUME...
AND THE JARS, TOO!
I ALERTED LEO'S MOM. SHE'S ALREADY MAKING MO-- OOPS!
THUD
OH, NOOO! NOW I'LL HAVE TO PICK THEM UP ONE BY ONE!
TIP TIP
TIP TIP TIP
DON'T WORRY! WE'RE ALL TIRED AND DESERVE A LITTLE BREAK! WE'LL STRAIGHTEN UP TOMORROW MORNING!
THANKS, LAVENDER!
WELL SAID! MY STOMACH NEEDS TO GET FILLED UP!
I'M SO WIPED OUT I COULD GO STRAIGHT TO BED!
IN THE DEAD OF NIGHT...
NO SECURITY LOCKS! IT'S NICE TO SEE THERE'RE STILL FOLKS THAT COUNT ON THEIR NEIGHBORS! HEE! HEE! HEE!
CLANK

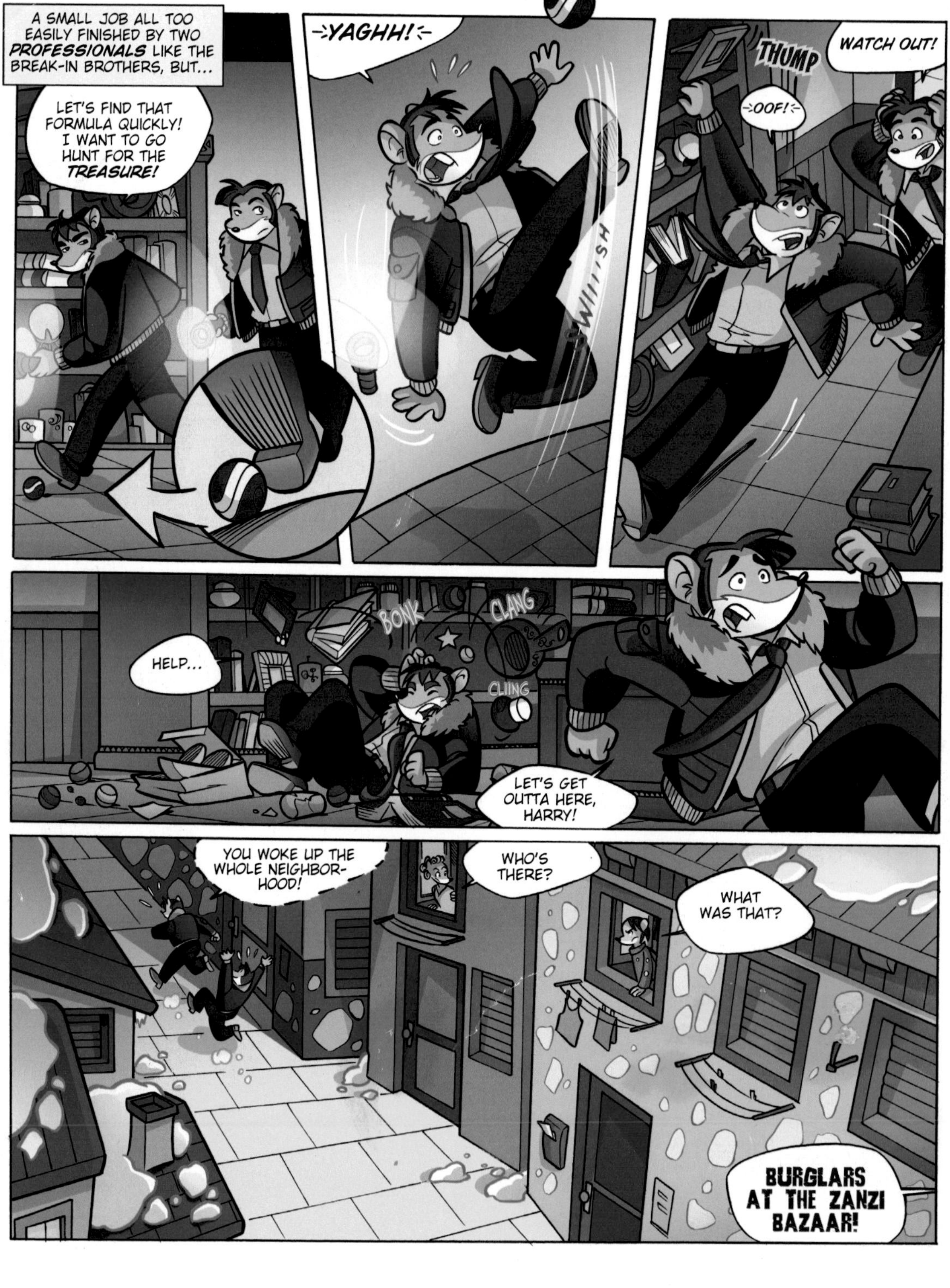
A SMALL JOB ALL TOO EASILY FINISHED BY TWO PROFESSIONALS LIKE THE BREAK-IN BROTHERS, BUT...
LET'S FIND THAT FORMULA QUICKLY! I WANT TO GO HUNT FOR THE TREASURE!
YAGHH!
WHIIISH
THUMP
WATCH OUT!
OOF!
BONK
CLANG
CLIING
HELP...
LET'S GET OUTTA HERE, HARRY!
YOU WOKE UP THE WHOLE NEIGHBOR-HOOD!
WHO'S THERE?
WHAT WAS THAT?
BURGLARS AT THE ZANZI BAZAAR!

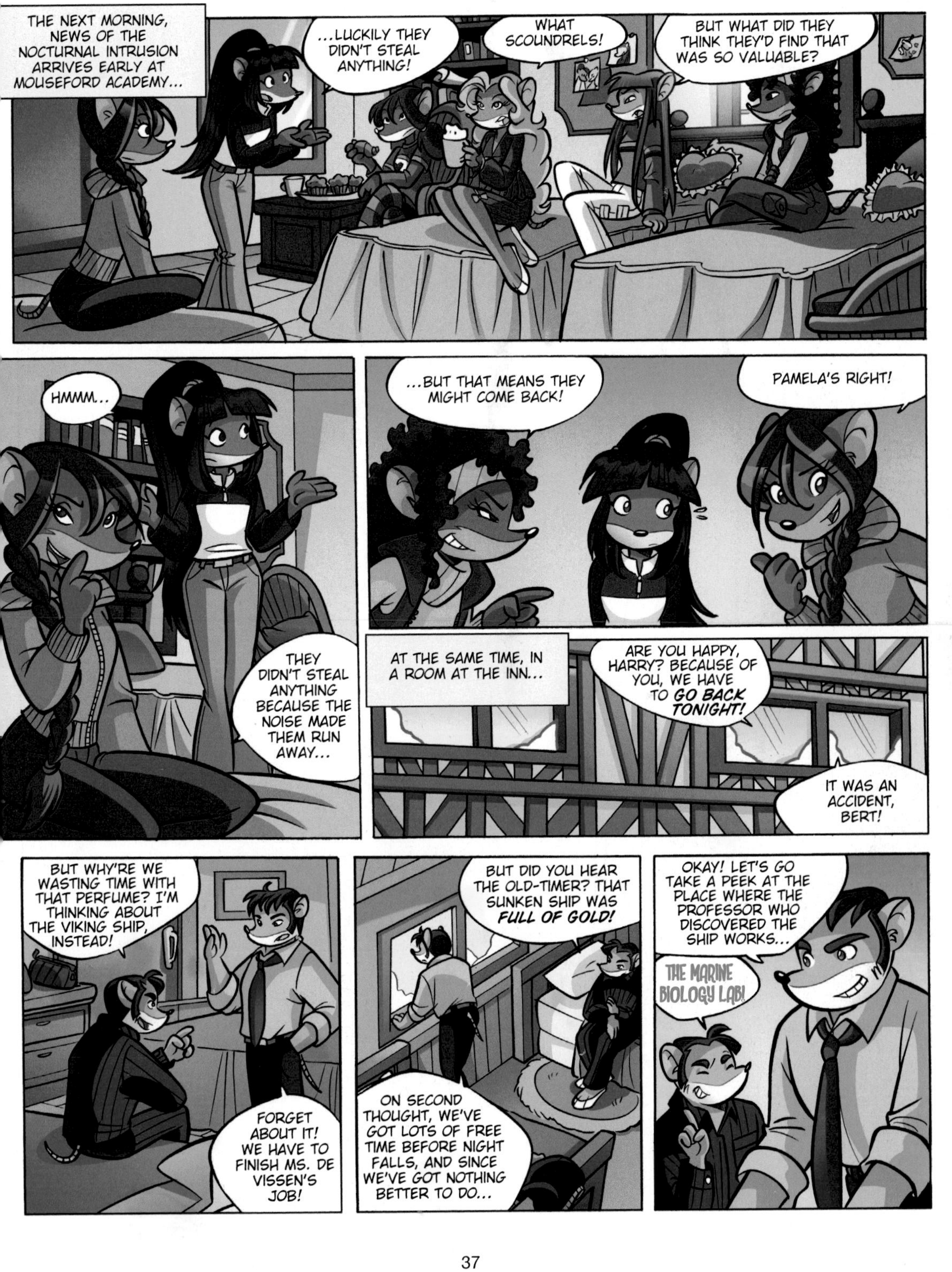

THE NEXT MORNING, NEWS OF THE NOCTURNAL INTRUSION ARRIVES EARLY AT MOUSEFORD ACADEMY...
...LUCKILY THEY DIDN'T STEAL ANYTHING!
WHAT SCOUNDRELS!
BUT WHAT DID THEY THINK THEY'D FIND THAT WAS SO VALUABLE?
HMMM...
THEY DIDN'T STEAL ANYTHING BECAUSE THE NOISE MADE THEM RUN AWAY...
...BUT THAT MEANS THEY MIGHT COME BACK!
PAMELA'S RIGHT!
AT THE SAME TIME, IN A ROOM AT THE INN...
ARE YOU HAPPY, HARRY? BECAUSE OF YOU, WE HAVE TO GO BACK TONIGHT!
IT WAS AN ACCIDENT, BERT!
BUT WHY'RE WE WASTING TIME WITH THAT PERFUME? I'M THINKING ABOUT THE VIKING SHIP, INSTEAD!
FORGET ABOUT IT! WE HAVE TO FINISH MS. DE VISSEN'S JOB!
BUT DID YOU HEAR THE OLD-TIMER? THAT SUNKEN SHIP WAS FULL OF GOLD!
ON SECOND THOUGHT, WE'VE GOT LOTS OF FREE TIME BEFORE NIGHT FALLS, AND SINCE WE'VE GOT NOTHING BETTER TO DO...
OKAY! LET'S GO TAKE A PEEK AT THE PLACE WHERE THE PROFESSOR WHO DISCOVERED THE SHIP WORKS...
THE MARINE BIOLOGY LAB!

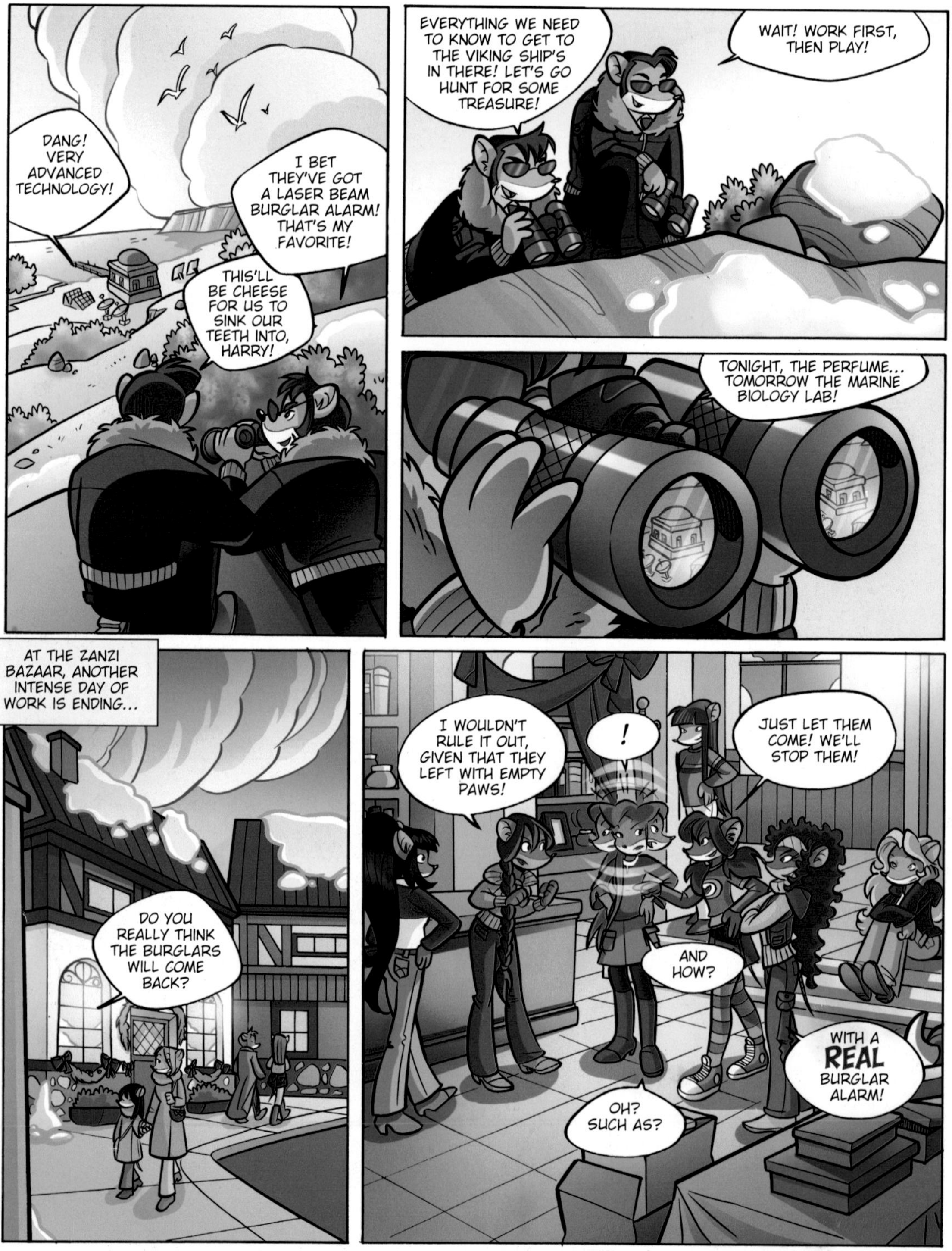
DANG! VERY ADVANCED TECHNOLOGY!
I BET THEY'VE GOT A LASER BEAM BURGLAR ALARM! THAT'S MY FAVORITE!
THIS'LL BE CHEESE FOR US TO SINK OUR TEETH INTO, HARRY!
EVERYTHING WE NEED TO KNOW TO GET TO THE VIKING SHIP'S IN THERE! LET'S GO HUNT FOR SOME TREASURE!
WAIT! WORK FIRST, THEN PLAY!
TONIGHT, THE PERFUME... TOMORROW THE MARINE BIOLOGY LAB!
AT THE ZANZI BAZAAR, ANOTHER INTENSE DAY OF WORK IS ENDING...
DO YOU REALLY THINK THE BURGLARS WILL COME BACK?
I WOULDN'T RULE IT OUT, GIVEN THAT THEY LEFT WITH EMPTY PAWS!
!
JUST LET THEM COME! WE'LL STOP THEM!
AND HOW?
WITH A REAL BURGLAR ALARM!
OH? SUCH AS?

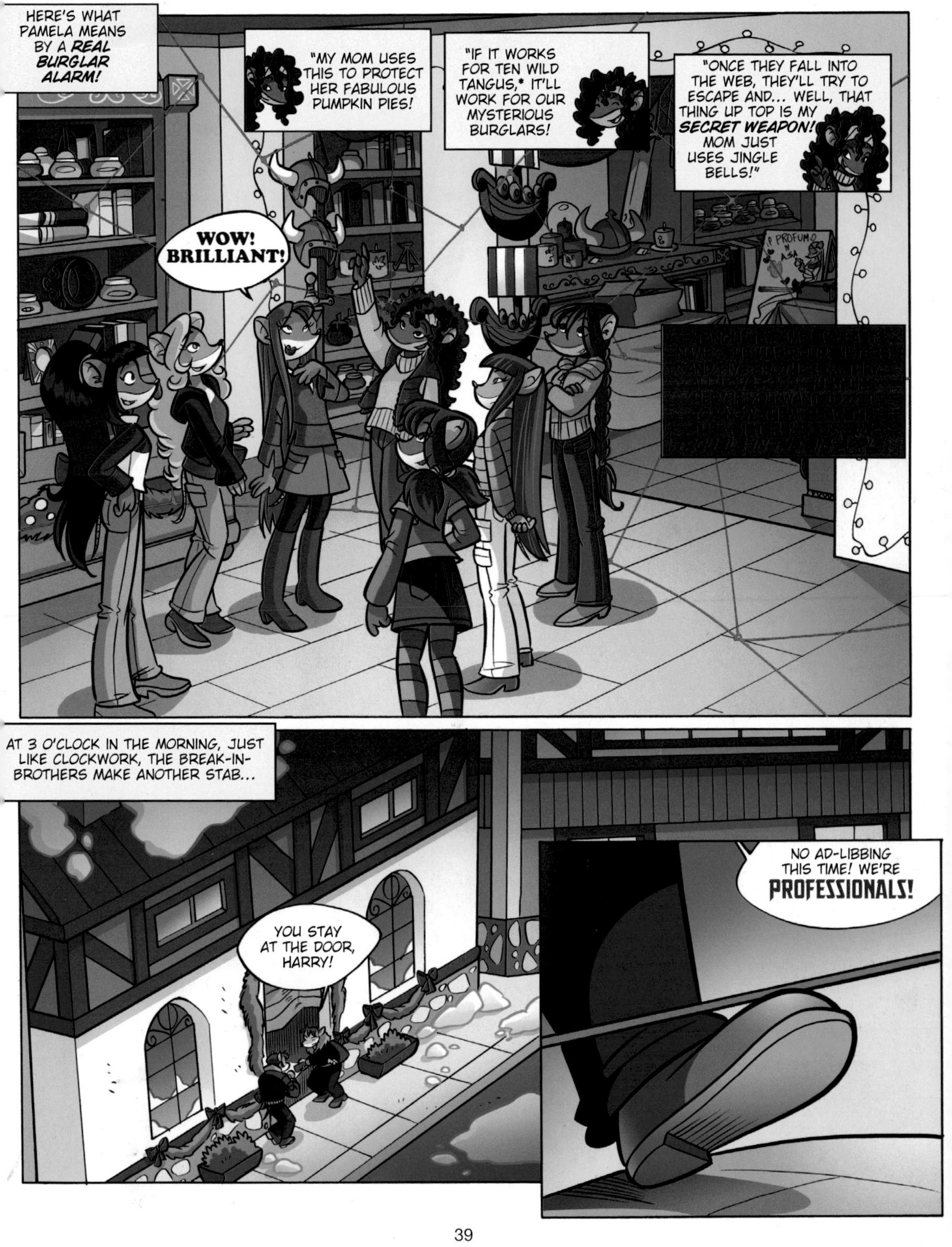
HERE'S WHAT PAMELA MEANS BY A REAL BURGLAR ALARM!
"MY MOM USES THIS TO PROTECT HER FABULOUS PUMPKIN PIES!
"IF IT WORKS FOR TEN WILD TANGUS,* IT'LL WORK FOR OUR MYSTERIOUS BURGLARS!
"ONCE THEY FALL INTO THE WEB, THEY'LL TRY TO ESCAPE AND... WELL, THAT THING UP TOP IS MY SECRET WEAPON! MOM JUST USES JINGLE BELLS!"
WOW! BRILLIANT!
[redacted]
AT 3 O'CLOCK IN THE MORNING, JUST LIKE CLOCKWORK, THE BREAK-IN-BROTHERS MAKE ANOTHER STAB...
YOU STAY AT THE DOOR, HARRY!
NO AD-LIBBING THIS TIME! WE'RE PROFESSIONALS!

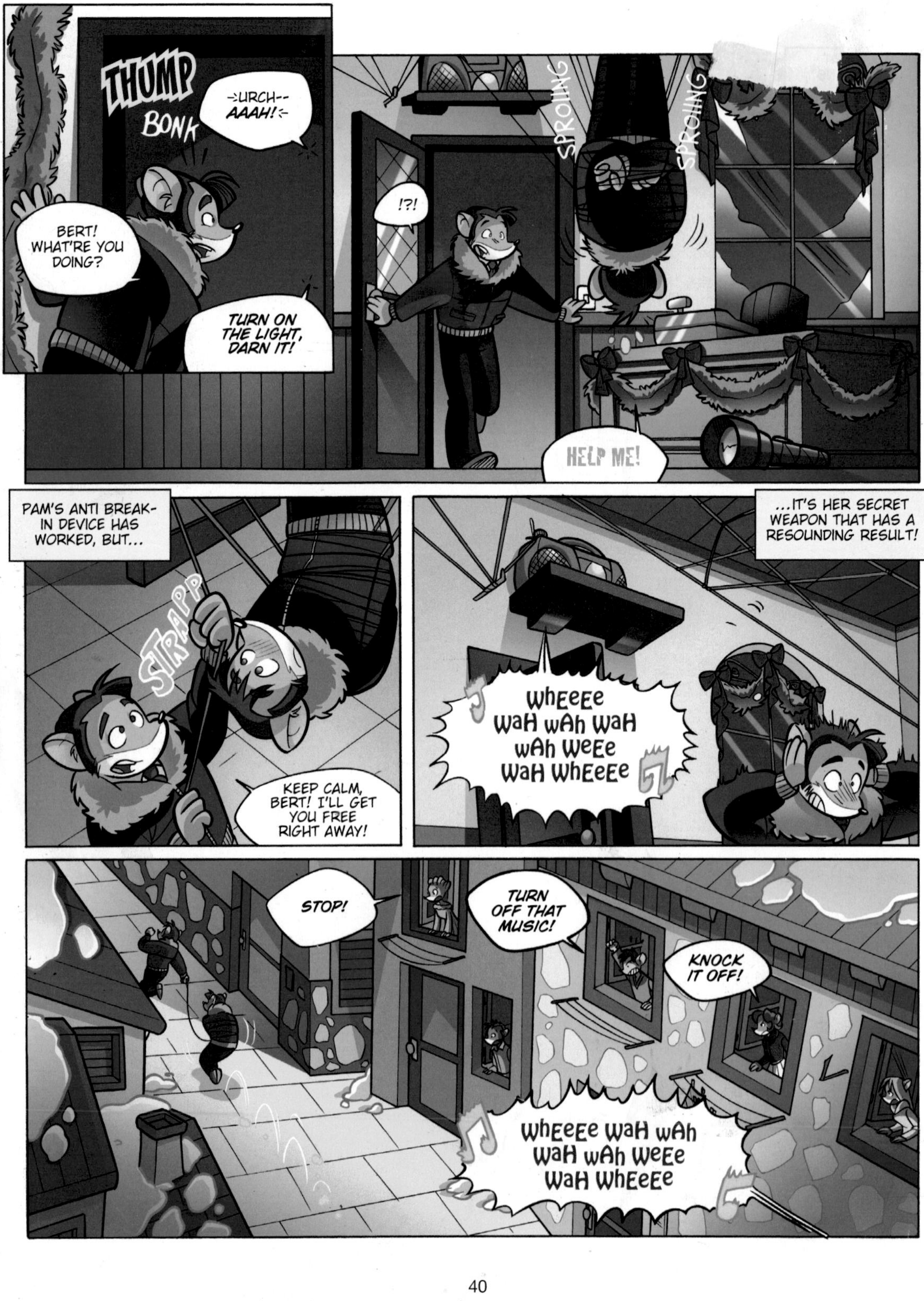
THUMP
BONK
URCH--
AAAH!
BERT! WHAT'RE YOU DOING?
TURN ON THE LIGHT, DARN IT!
!?!
SPROIING
SPROIING
HELP ME!
PAM'S ANTI BREAK-IN DEVICE HAS WORKED, BUT...
STRAPP
KEEP CALM, BERT! I'LL GET YOU FREE RIGHT AWAY!
...IT'S HER SECRET WEAPON THAT HAS A RESOUNDING RESULT!
WhEEEE WaH wAh WaH wAh WEEe WaH WhEEEE
STOP!
TURN OFF THAT MUSIC!
KNOCK IT OFF!
WhEEEE WaH wAh WaH wAh WEEe WaH WhEEEE

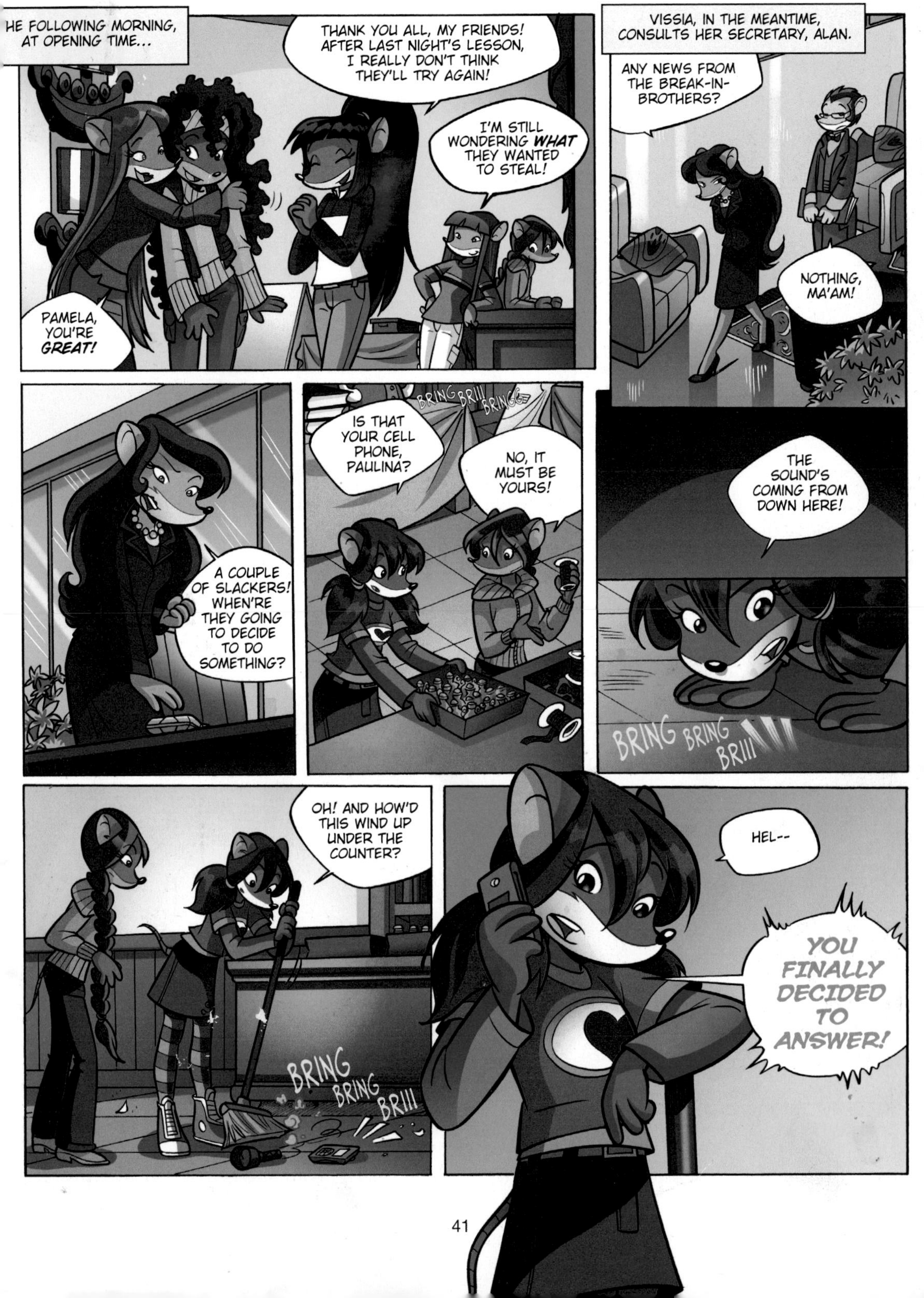
HE FOLLOWING MORNING, AT OPENING TIME...
THANK YOU ALL, MY FRIENDS! AFTER LAST NIGHT'S LESSON, I REALLY DON'T THINK THEY'LL TRY AGAIN!
I'M STILL WONDERING WHAT THEY WANTED TO STEAL!
PAMELA, YOU'RE GREAT!
VISSIA, IN THE MEANTIME, CONSULTS HER SECRETARY, ALAN.
ANY NEWS FROM THE BREAK-IN-BROTHERS?
NOTHING, MA'AM!
A COUPLE OF SLACKERS! WHEN'RE THEY GOING TO DECIDE TO DO SOMETHING?
BRING BRIII BRINGG
IS THAT YOUR CELL PHONE, PAULINA?
NO, IT MUST BE YOURS!
THE SOUND'S COMING FROM DOWN HERE!
BRING BRING BRIII
OH! AND HOW'D THIS WIND UP UNDER THE COUNTER?
BRING BRING BRIII
HEL--
YOU FINALLY DECIDED TO ANSWER!

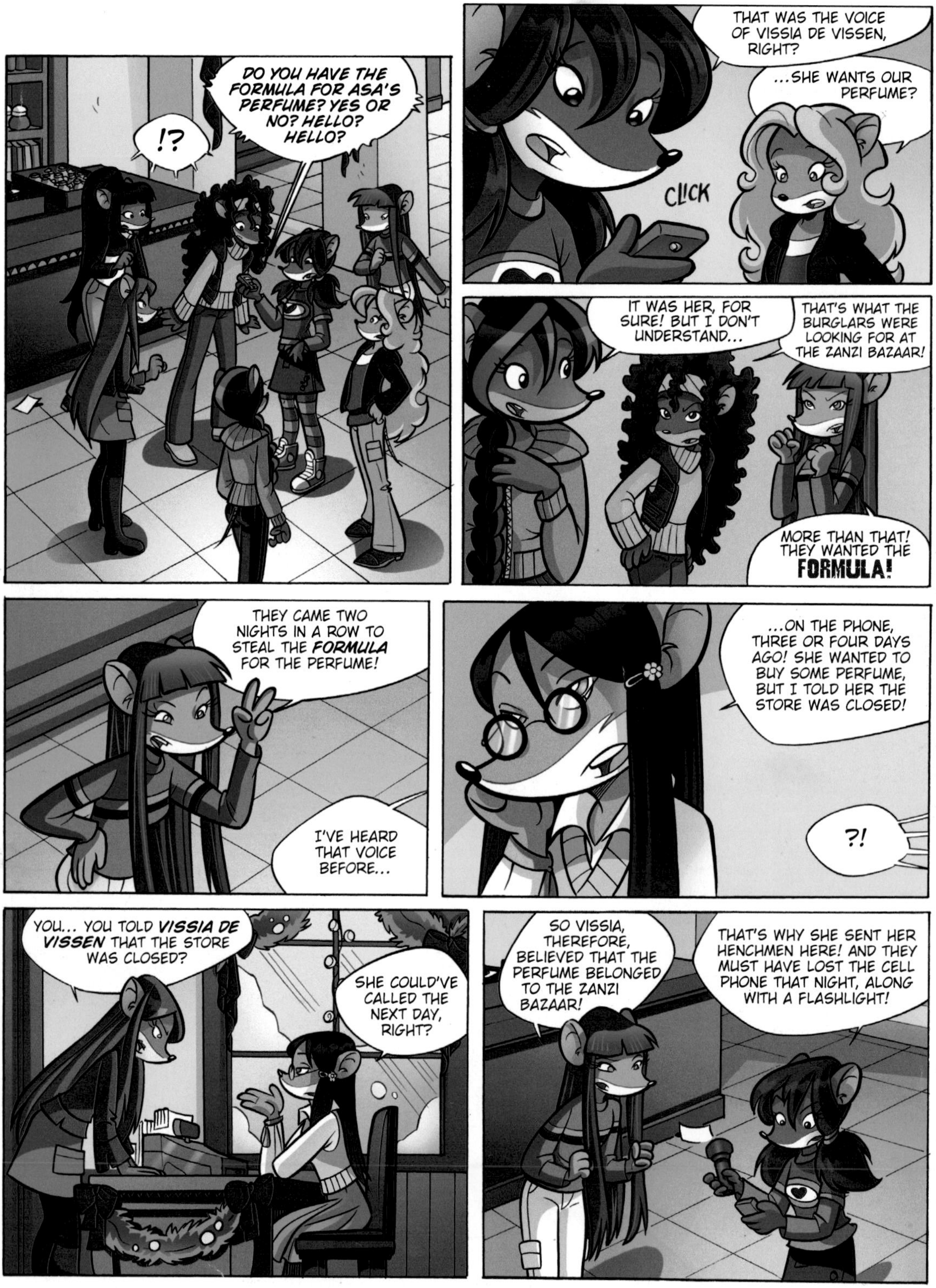

!?
DO YOU HAVE THE FORMULA FOR ASA'S PERFUME? YES OR NO? HELLO? HELLO?
THAT WAS THE VOICE OF VISSIA DE VISSEN, RIGHT?
...SHE WANTS OUR PERFUME?
CLICK
IT WAS HER, FOR SURE! BUT I DON'T UNDERSTAND...
THAT'S WHAT THE BURGLARS WERE LOOKING FOR AT THE ZANZI BAZAAR!
MORE THAN THAT! THEY WANTED THE FORMULA!
THEY CAME TWO NIGHTS IN A ROW TO STEAL THE FORMULA FOR THE PERFUME!
I'VE HEARD THAT VOICE BEFORE...
...ON THE PHONE, THREE OR FOUR DAYS AGO! SHE WANTED TO BUY SOME PERFUME, BUT I TOLD HER THE STORE WAS CLOSED!
?!
YOU... YOU TOLD VISSIA DE VISSEN THAT THE STORE WAS CLOSED?
SHE COULD'VE CALLED THE NEXT DAY, RIGHT?
SO VISSIA, THEREFORE, BELIEVED THAT THE PERFUME BELONGED TO THE ZANZI BAZAAR!
THAT'S WHY SHE SENT HER HENCHMEN HERE! AND THEY MUST HAVE LOST THE CELL PHONE THAT NIGHT, ALONG WITH A FLASHLIGHT!

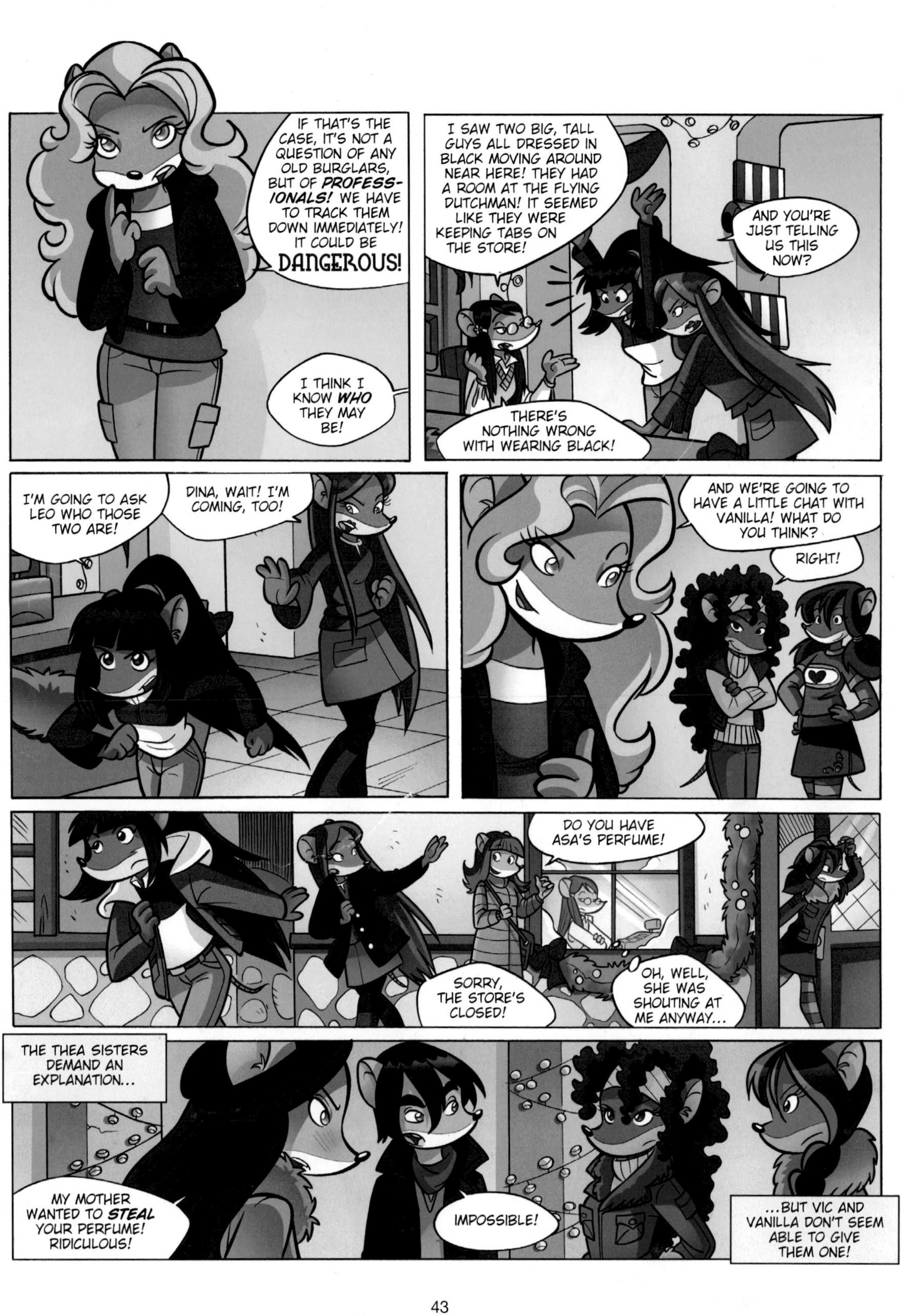
IF THAT'S THE CASE, IT'S NOT A QUESTION OF ANY OLD BURGLARS, BUT OF PROFESSIONALS! WE HAVE TO TRACK THEM DOWN IMMEDIATELY! IT COULD BE DANGEROUS!
I THINK I KNOW WHO THEY MAY BE!
I SAW TWO BIG, TALL GUYS ALL DRESSED IN BLACK MOVING AROUND NEAR HERE! THEY HAD A ROOM AT THE FLYING DUTCHMAN! IT SEEMED LIKE THEY WERE KEEPING TABS ON THE STORE!
AND YOU'RE JUST TELLING US THIS NOW?
THERE'S NOTHING WRONG WITH WEARING BLACK!
I'M GOING TO ASK LEO WHO THOSE TWO ARE!
DINA, WAIT! I'M COMING, TOO!
AND WE'RE GOING TO HAVE A LITTLE CHAT WITH VANILLA! WHAT DO YOU THINK?
RIGHT!
DO YOU HAVE ASA'S PERFUME!
SORRY, THE STORE'S CLOSED!
OH, WELL, SHE WAS SHOUTING AT ME ANYWAY...
THE THEA SISTERS DEMAND AN EXPLANATION...
MY MOTHER WANTED TO STEAL YOUR PERFUME! RIDICULOUS!
IMPOSSIBLE!
...BUT VIC AND VANILLA DON'T SEEM ABLE TO GIVE THEM ONE!

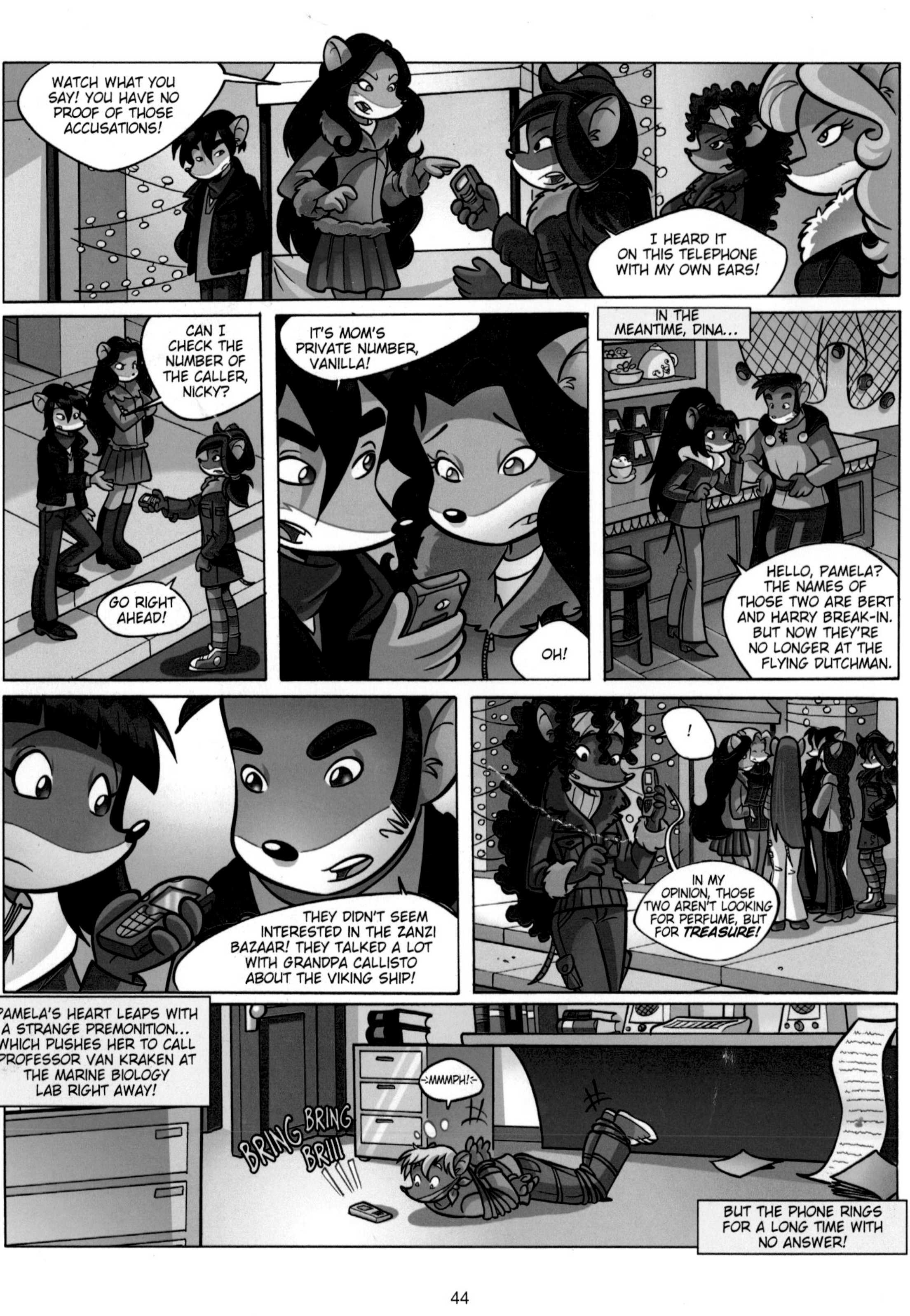
WATCH WHAT YOU SAY! YOU HAVE NO PROOF OF THOSE ACCUSATIONS!
I HEARD IT ON THIS TELEPHONE WITH MY OWN EARS!
CAN I CHECK THE NUMBER OF THE CALLER, NICKY?
GO RIGHT AHEAD!
IT'S MOM'S PRIVATE NUMBER, VANILLA!
OH!
IN THE MEANTIME, DINA...
HELLO, PAMELA? THE NAMES OF THOSE TWO ARE BERT AND HARRY BREAK-IN. BUT NOW THEY'RE NO LONGER AT THE FLYING DUTCHMAN.
THEY DIDN'T SEEM INTERESTED IN THE ZANZI BAZAAR! THEY TALKED A LOT WITH GRANDPA CALLISTO ABOUT THE VIKING SHIP!
!
IN MY OPINION, THOSE TWO AREN'T LOOKING FOR PERFUME, BUT FOR TREASURE!
PAMELA'S HEART LEAPS WITH A STRANGE PREMONITION... WHICH PUSHES HER TO CALL PROFESSOR VAN KRAKEN AT THE MARINE BIOLOGY LAB RIGHT AWAY!
MMMPH!
BRING BRING BRIII
BUT THE PHONE RINGS FOR A LONG TIME WITH NO ANSWER!

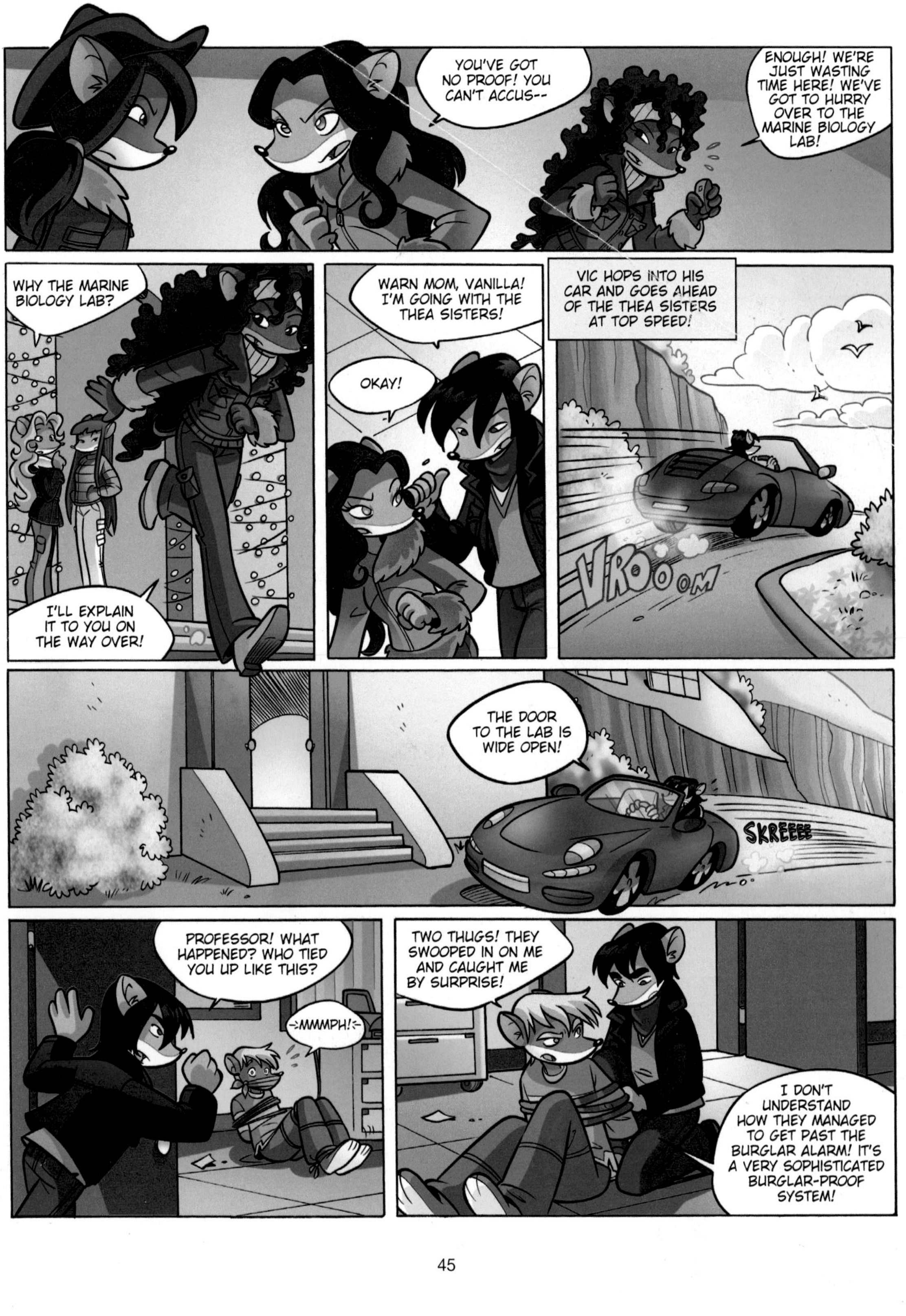
YOU'VE GOT NO PROOF! YOU CAN'T ACCUS--
ENOUGH! WE'RE JUST WASTING TIME HERE! WE'VE GOT TO HURRY OVER TO THE MARINE BIOLOGY LAB!
WHY THE MARINE BIOLOGY LAB?
I'LL EXPLAIN IT TO YOU ON THE WAY OVER!
WARN MOM, VANILLA! I'M GOING WITH THE THEA SISTERS!
OKAY!
VIC HOPS INTO HIS CAR AND GOES AHEAD OF THE THEA SISTERS AT TOP SPEED!
VROOOM
THE DOOR TO THE LAB IS WIDE OPEN!
SKREEEE
PROFESSOR! WHAT HAPPENED? WHO TIED YOU UP LIKE THIS?
-MMMPH!-
TWO THUGS! THEY SWOOPED IN ON ME AND CAUGHT ME BY SURPRISE!
I DON'T UNDERSTAND HOW THEY MANAGED TO GET PAST THE BURGLAR ALARM! IT'S A VERY SOPHISTICATED BURGLAR-PROOF SYSTEM!

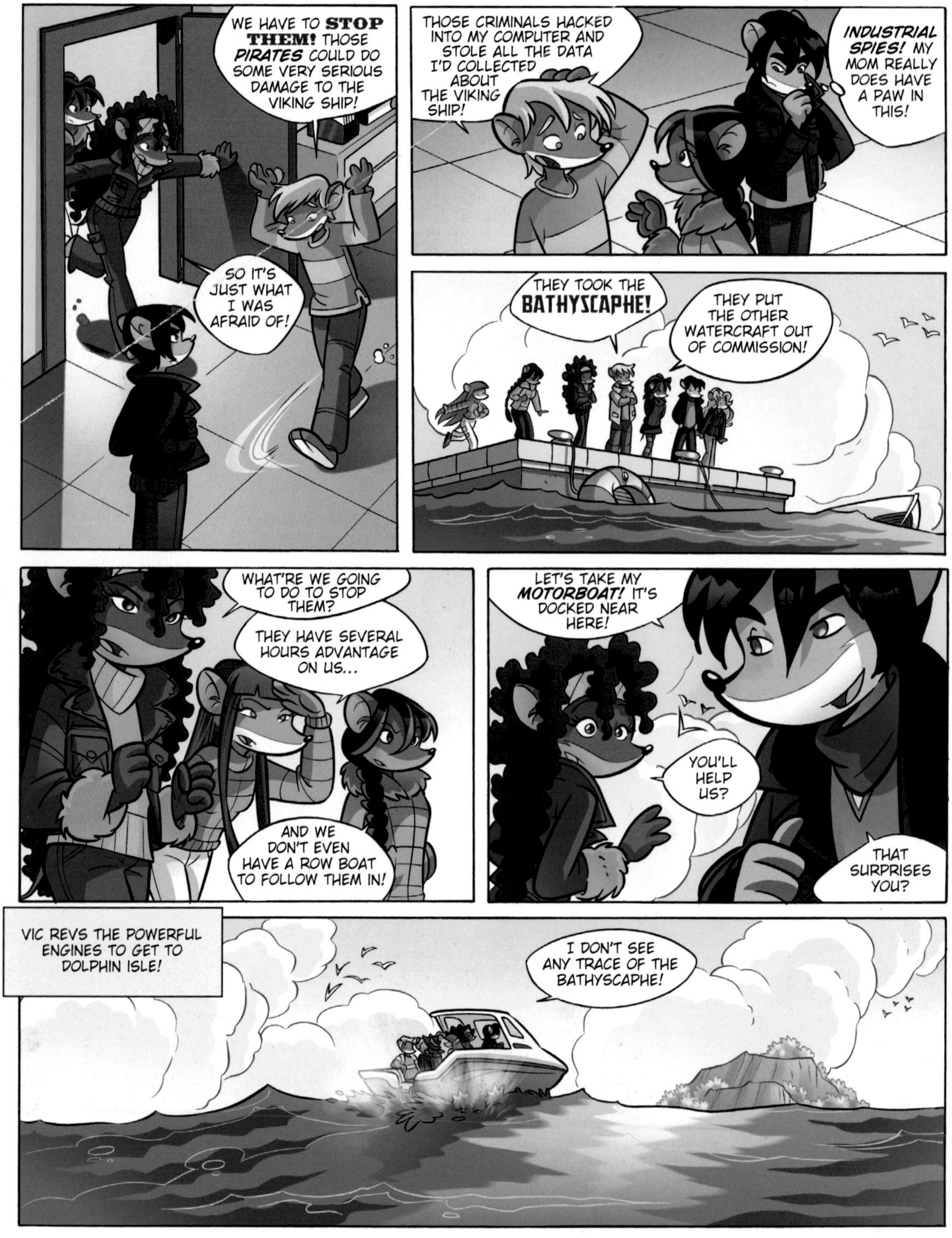
WE HAVE TO STOP THEM! THOSE PIRATES COULD DO SOME VERY SERIOUS DAMAGE TO THE VIKING SHIP!
SO IT'S JUST WHAT I WAS AFRAID OF!
THOSE CRIMINALS HACKED INTO MY COMPUTER AND STOLE ALL THE DATA I'D COLLECTED ABOUT THE VIKING SHIP!
INDUSTRIAL SPIES! MY MOM REALLY DOES HAVE A PAW IN THIS!
THEY TOOK THE BATHYSCAPHE!
THEY PUT THE OTHER WATERCRAFT OUT OF COMMISSION!
WHAT'RE WE GOING TO DO TO STOP THEM?
THEY HAVE SEVERAL HOURS ADVANTAGE ON US...
AND WE DON'T EVEN HAVE A ROW BOAT TO FOLLOW THEM IN!
LET'S TAKE MY MOTORBOAT! IT'S DOCKED NEAR HERE!
YOU'LL HELP US?
THAT SURPRISES YOU?
VIC REVS THE POWERFUL ENGINES TO GET TO DOLPHIN ISLE!
I DON'T SEE ANY TRACE OF THE BATHYSCAPHE!

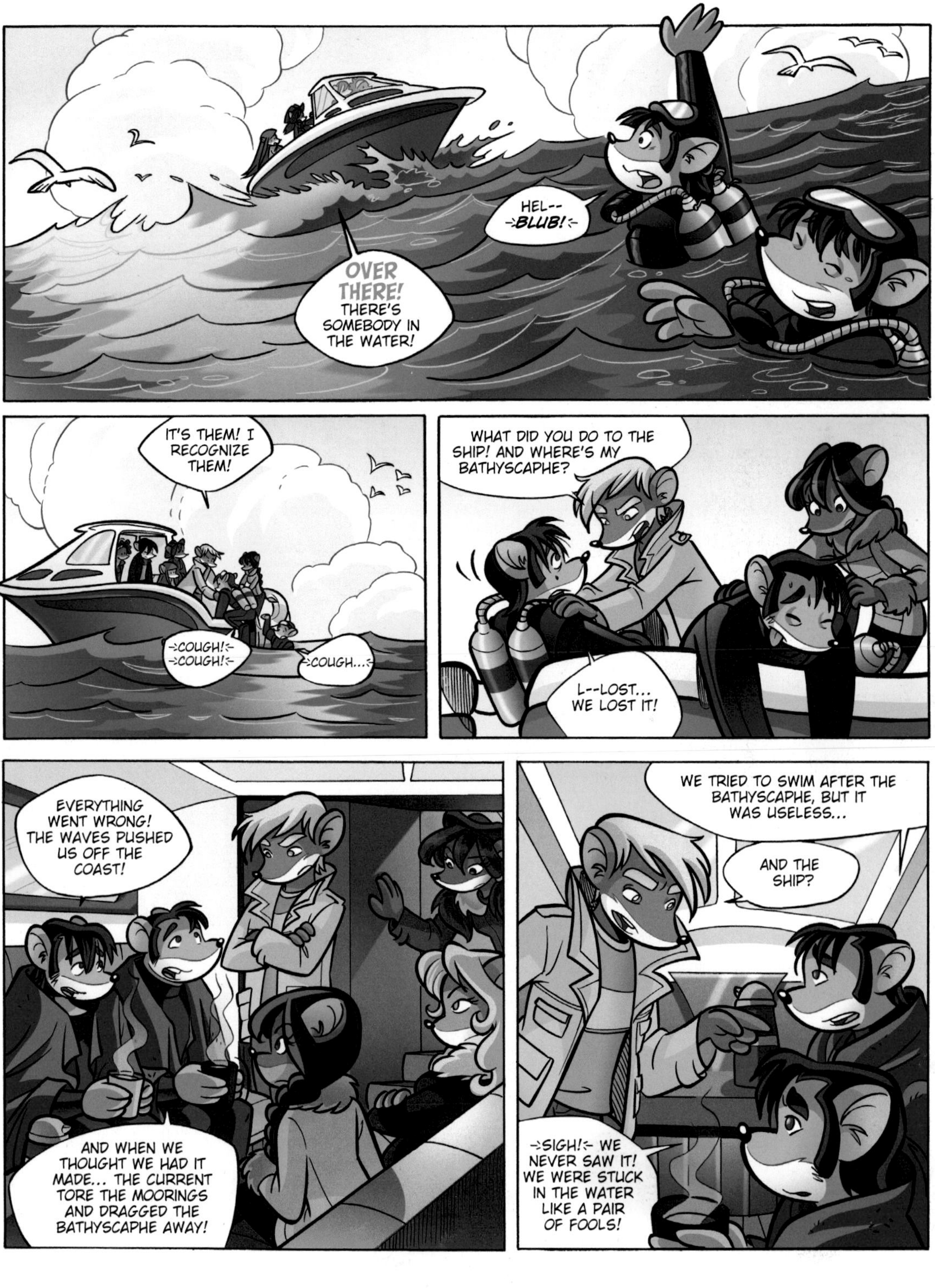
OVER THERE! THERE'S SOMEBODY IN THE WATER!
HEL-- -BLUB!-
IT'S THEM! I RECOGNIZE THEM!
-COUGH!- -COUGH!-
-COUGH...-
WHAT DID YOU DO TO THE SHIP! AND WHERE'S MY BATHYSCAPHE?
L--LOST... WE LOST IT!
EVERYTHING WENT WRONG! THE WAVES PUSHED US OFF THE COAST!
AND WHEN WE THOUGHT WE HAD IT MADE... THE CURRENT TORE THE MOORINGS AND DRAGGED THE BATHYSCAPHE AWAY!
WE TRIED TO SWIM AFTER THE BATHYSCAPHE, BUT IT WAS USELESS...
AND THE SHIP?
-SIGH!- WE NEVER SAW IT! WE WERE STUCK IN THE WATER LIKE A PAIR OF FOOLS!

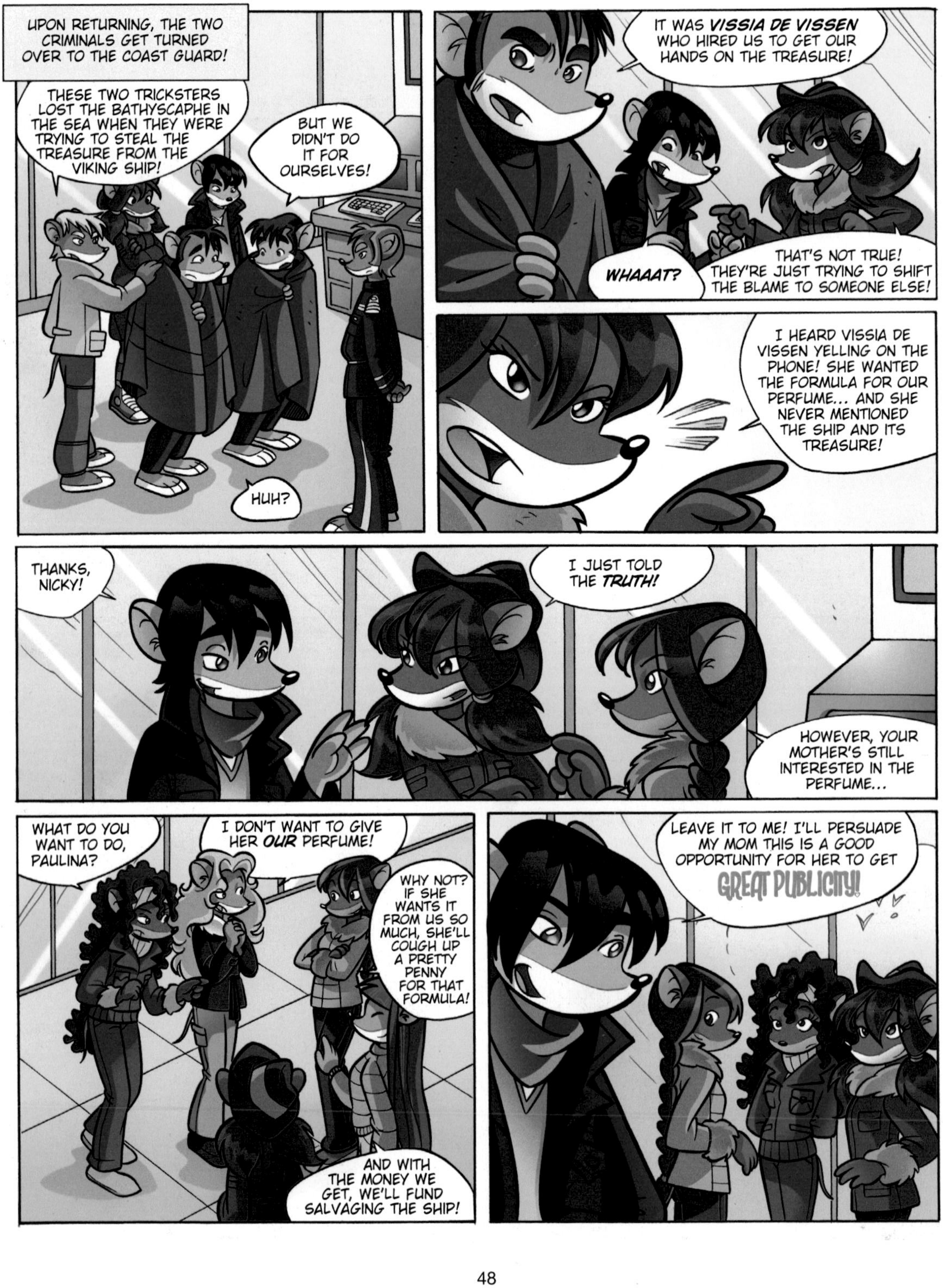
UPON RETURNING, THE TWO CRIMINALS GET TURNED OVER TO THE COAST GUARD!
THESE TWO TRICKSTERS LOST THE BATHYSCAPHE IN THE SEA WHEN THEY WERE TRYING TO STEAL THE TREASURE FROM THE VIKING SHIP!
BUT WE DIDN'T DO IT FOR OURSELVES!
HUH?
IT WAS VISSIA DE VISSEN WHO HIRED US TO GET OUR HANDS ON THE TREASURE!
WHAAAT?
THAT'S NOT TRUE! THEY'RE JUST TRYING TO SHIFT THE BLAME TO SOMEONE ELSE!
I HEARD VISSIA DE VISSEN YELLING ON THE PHONE! SHE WANTED THE FORMULA FOR OUR PERFUME... AND SHE NEVER MENTIONED THE SHIP AND ITS TREASURE!
THANKS, NICKY!
I JUST TOLD THE TRUTH!
HOWEVER, YOUR MOTHER'S STILL INTERESTED IN THE PERFUME...
WHAT DO YOU WANT TO DO, PAULINA?
I DON'T WANT TO GIVE HER OUR PERFUME!
WHY NOT? IF SHE WANTS IT FROM US SO MUCH, SHE'LL COUGH UP A PRETTY PENNY FOR THAT FORMULA!
AND WITH THE MONEY WE GET, WE'LL FUND SALVAGING THE SHIP!
LEAVE IT TO ME! I'LL PERSUADE MY MOM THIS IS A GOOD OPPORTUNITY FOR HER TO GET
GREAT PUBLICITY!

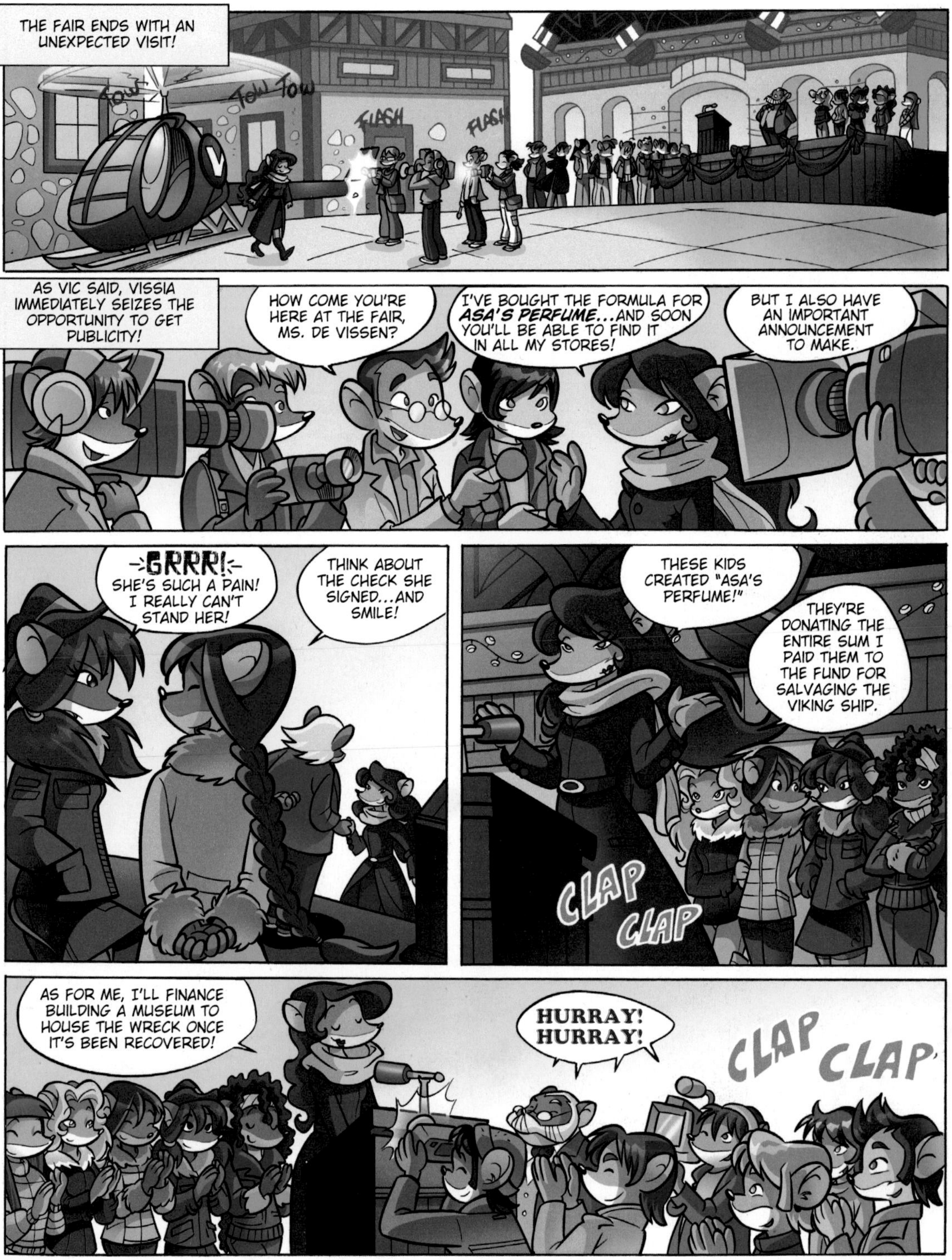
THE FAIR ENDS WITH AN UNEXPECTED VISIT!
TOW TOW TOW
FLASH
FLASH
AS VIC SAID, VISSIA IMMEDIATELY SEIZES THE OPPORTUNITY TO GET PUBLICITY!
HOW COME YOU'RE HERE AT THE FAIR, MS. DE VISSEN?
I'VE BOUGHT THE FORMULA FOR ASA'S PERFUME...AND SOON YOU'LL BE ABLE TO FIND IT IN ALL MY STORES!
BUT I ALSO HAVE AN IMPORTANT ANNOUNCEMENT TO MAKE.
GRRR! SHE'S SUCH A PAIN! I REALLY CAN'T STAND HER!
THINK ABOUT THE CHECK SHE SIGNED...AND SMILE!
THESE KIDS CREATED "ASA'S PERFUME!"
THEY'RE DONATING THE ENTIRE SUM I PAID THEM TO THE FUND FOR SALVAGING THE VIKING SHIP.
CLAP CLAP
AS FOR ME, I'LL FINANCE BUILDING A MUSEUM TO HOUSE THE WRECK ONCE IT'S BEEN RECOVERED!
HURRAY! HURRAY!
CLAP CLAP

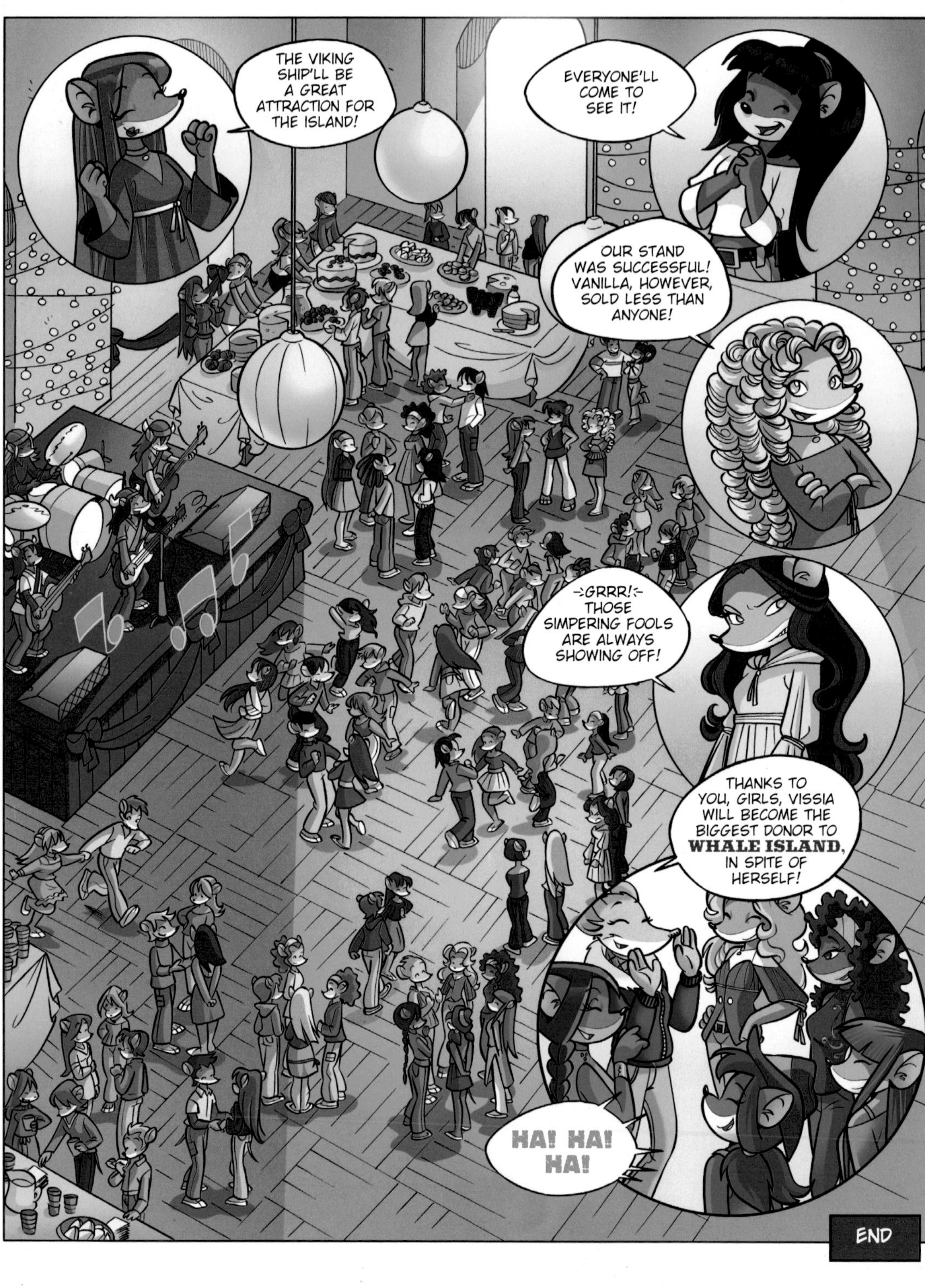
THE VIKING SHIP'LL BE A GREAT ATTRACTION FOR THE ISLAND!
EVERYONE'LL COME TO SEE IT!
OUR STAND WAS SUCCESSFUL! VANILLA, HOWEVER, SOLD LESS THAN ANYONE!
GRRR! THOSE SIMPERING FOOLS ARE ALWAYS SHOWING OFF!
THANKS TO YOU, GIRLS, VISSIA WILL BECOME THE BIGGEST DONOR TO WHALE ISLAND, IN SPITE OF HERSELF!
HA! HA! HA!
END

Watch Out For PAPERCUTZ™

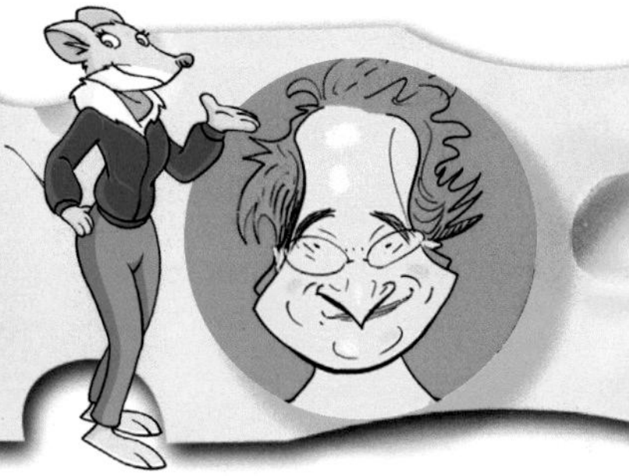

Welcome to the treasure-laden third THEA STILTON graphic novel from Papercutz, the folks dedicated to publishing great graphic novels for all ages. I'm Salicrup, *Jim Salicrup*, Editor-in-Chief and unofficial Mouseford Academy Truant Officer.

Instead of me yapping about THEA STILTON or the many other wonderful Papercutz titles available to you, let's just play a little game shall we? Just draw a line between the pictured Thea Sister or other Papercutz character on the left with their correct name on the right. It's that easy! Answers are printed upside-down at the bottom of this page in teeny-tiny type.

Oh, and don't forget to look out for THEA STILTON #4 "Catching the Giant Wave," coming soon. Check out the preview on the following pages.

Class dismissed!

Thanks,

Jim

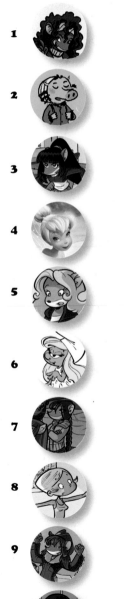

1 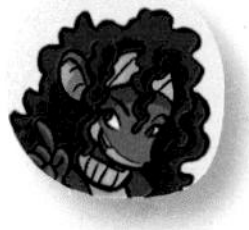

2 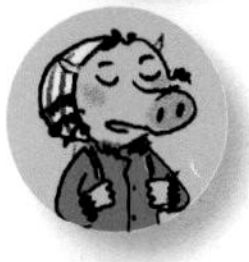

3 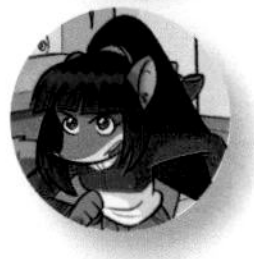

4 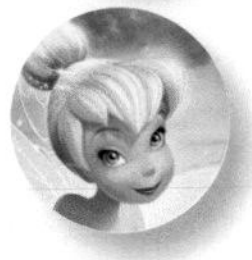

5 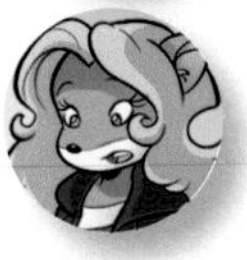

6 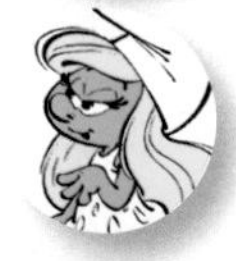

7 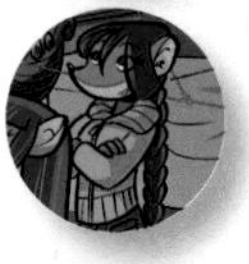

8 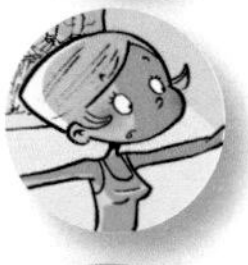

9 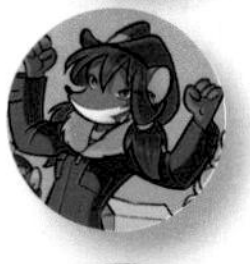

10 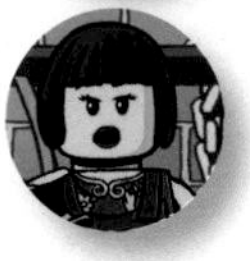

A – Paulina

B – Nya (From LEGO ® NINJAGO, she's a ninja!)

C – Pamela

D – Petula (From ARIOL, she's Ariol's secret love!)

E – Smurfette (From THE SMURFS, she's a female Smurf!)

F – Colette

G – Nicky

H – Julie (From DANCE CLASS, she's a dance student!)

I – Tinker Bell (From DISNEY FAIRIES, she's a fairy!)

J – Violet

Stay in Touch!

EMAIL:	salicrup@papercutz.com
WEB:	www.papercutz.com
TWITTER:	@papercutzgn
FACEBOOK:	PAPERCUTZGRAPHICNOVELS
FAN MAIL:	Papercutz, 160 Broadway, Suite 700, East Wing, New York, NY 10038

Caricature of Jim by Steve Brodner at the MoCCA Art Fest.

ANSWERS: 1-C, 2-D, 3-J, 4-I, 5-F, 6-E, 7-A, 8-H, 9-G, 10-B

Special Preview of THEA STILTON #4 "Catching the Giant Wave!"

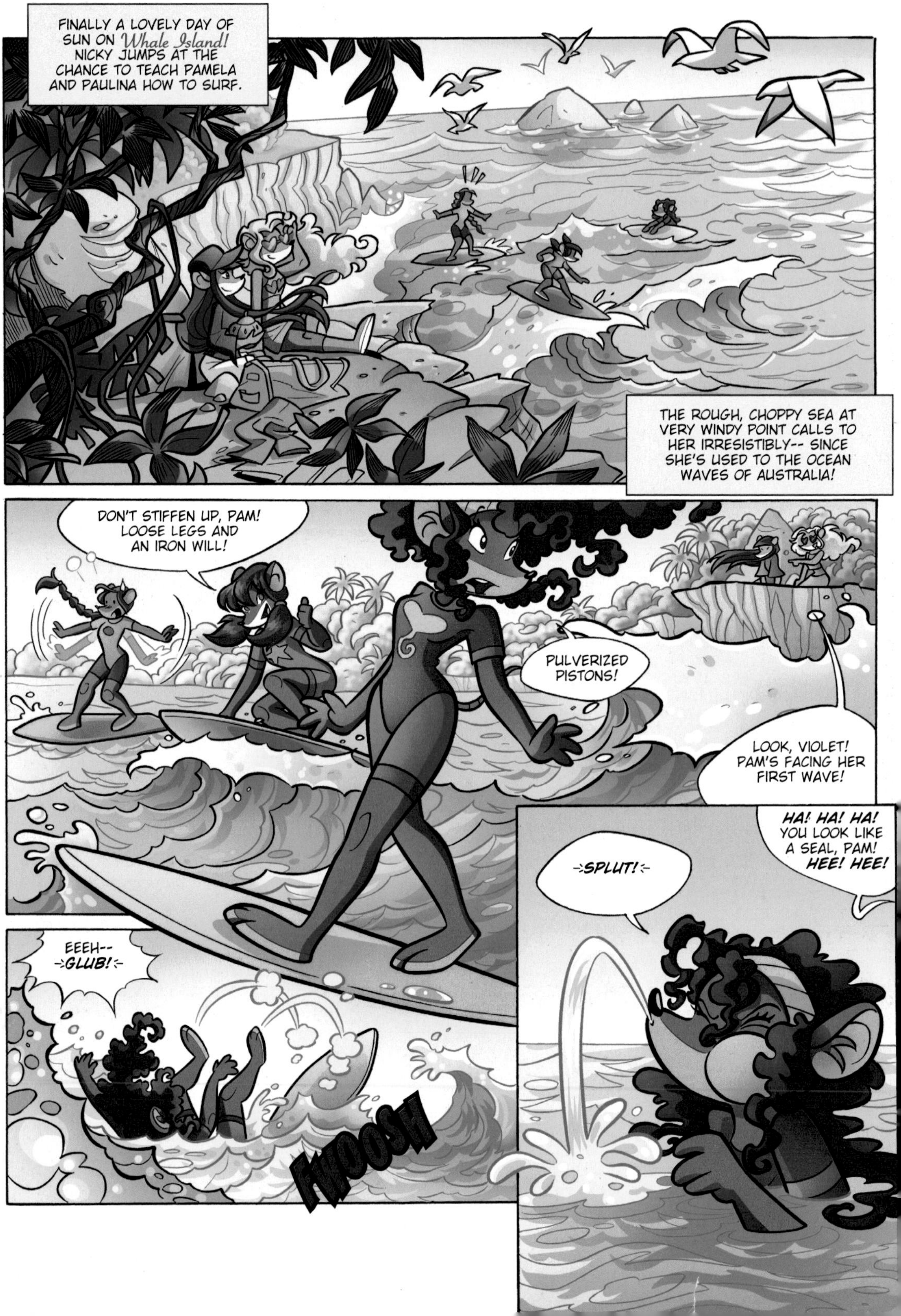
FINALLY A LOVELY DAY OF SUN ON Whale Island! NICKY JUMPS AT THE CHANCE TO TEACH PAMELA AND PAULINA HOW TO SURF.
THE ROUGH, CHOPPY SEA AT VERY WINDY POINT CALLS TO HER IRRESISTIBLY-- SINCE SHE'S USED TO THE OCEAN WAVES OF AUSTRALIA!
DON'T STIFFEN UP, PAM! LOOSE LEGS AND AN IRON WILL!
PULVERIZED PISTONS!
LOOK, VIOLET! PAM'S FACING HER FIRST WAVE!
EEEH-- -GLUB!-
FWOOSH
-SPLUT!-
HA! HA! HA! YOU LOOK LIKE A SEAL, PAM! HEE! HEE!

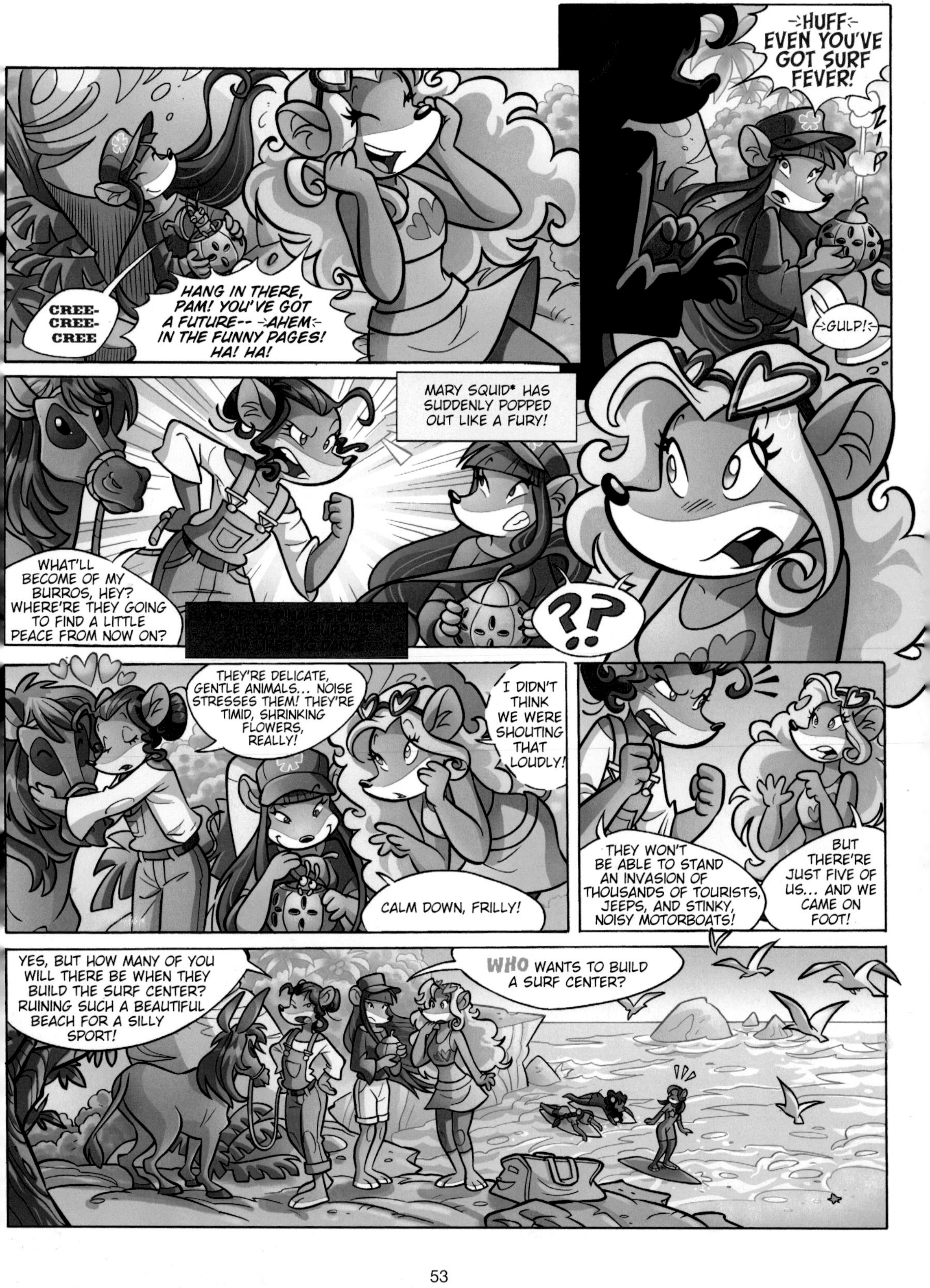
CREE-
CREE-
CREE
HANG IN THERE, PAM! YOU'VE GOT A FUTURE-- -AHEM- IN THE FUNNY PAGES! HA! HA!
-HUFF- EVEN YOU'VE GOT SURF FEVER!
ZIP
-GULP!-
MARY SQUID* HAS SUDDENLY POPPED OUT LIKE A FURY!
WHAT'LL BECOME OF MY BURROS, HEY? WHERE'RE THEY GOING TO FIND A LITTLE PEACE FROM NOW ON?
[redacted]
??
THEY'RE DELICATE, GENTLE ANIMALS... NOISE STRESSES THEM! THEY'RE TIMID, SHRINKING FLOWERS, REALLY!
I DIDN'T THINK WE WERE SHOUTING THAT LOUDLY!
CALM DOWN, FRILLY!
THEY WON'T BE ABLE TO STAND AN INVASION OF THOUSANDS OF TOURISTS, JEEPS, AND STINKY, NOISY MOTORBOATS!
BUT THERE'RE JUST FIVE OF US... AND WE CAME ON FOOT!
YES, BUT HOW MANY OF YOU WILL THERE BE WHEN THEY BUILD THE SURF CENTER? RUINING SUCH A BEAUTIFUL BEACH FOR A SILLY SPORT!
WHO WANTS TO BUILD A SURF CENTER?

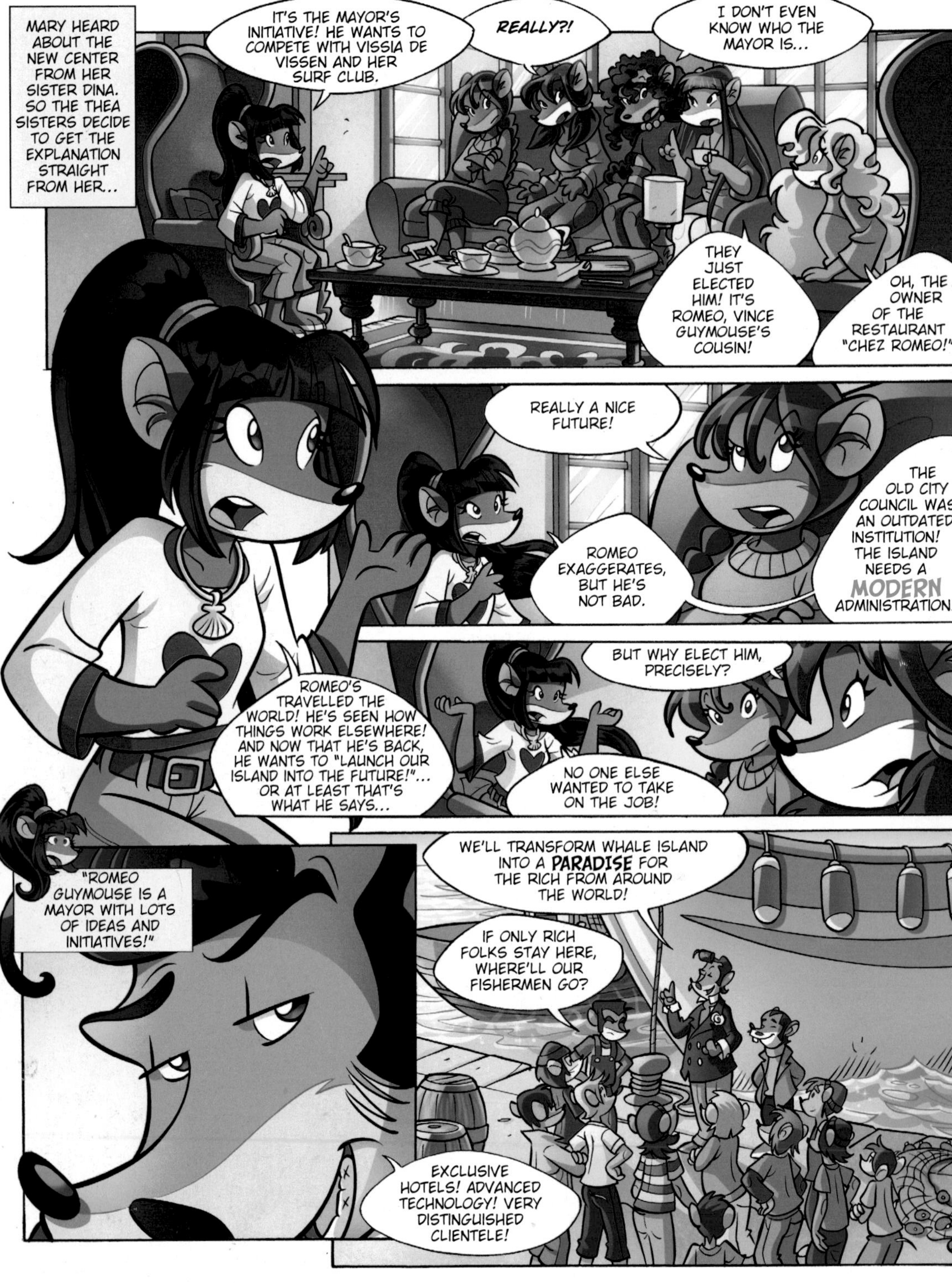
MARY HEARD ABOUT THE NEW CENTER FROM HER SISTER DINA. SO THE THEA SISTERS DECIDE TO GET THE EXPLANATION STRAIGHT FROM HER...
IT'S THE MAYOR'S INITIATIVE! HE WANTS TO COMPETE WITH VISSIA DE VISSEN AND HER SURF CLUB.
REALLY?!
I DON'T EVEN KNOW WHO THE MAYOR IS...
THEY JUST ELECTED HIM! IT'S ROMEO, VINCE GUYMOUSE'S COUSIN!
OH, THE OWNER OF THE RESTAURANT "CHEZ ROMEO!"
REALLY A NICE FUTURE!
ROMEO EXAGGERATES, BUT HE'S NOT BAD.
THE OLD CITY COUNCIL WAS AN OUTDATED INSTITUTION! THE ISLAND NEEDS A MODERN ADMINISTRATION!
BUT WHY ELECT HIM, PRECISELY?
NO ONE ELSE WANTED TO TAKE ON THE JOB!
ROMEO'S TRAVELLED THE WORLD! HE'S SEEN HOW THINGS WORK ELSEWHERE! AND NOW THAT HE'S BACK, HE WANTS TO "LAUNCH OUR ISLAND INTO THE FUTURE!"... OR AT LEAST THAT'S WHAT HE SAYS...
"ROMEO GUYMOUSE IS A MAYOR WITH LOTS OF IDEAS AND INITIATIVES!"
WE'LL TRANSFORM WHALE ISLAND INTO A PARADISE FOR THE RICH FROM AROUND THE WORLD!
IF ONLY RICH FOLKS STAY HERE, WHERE'LL OUR FISHERMEN GO?
EXCLUSIVE HOTELS! ADVANCED TECHNOLOGY! VERY DISTINGUISHED CLIENTELE!

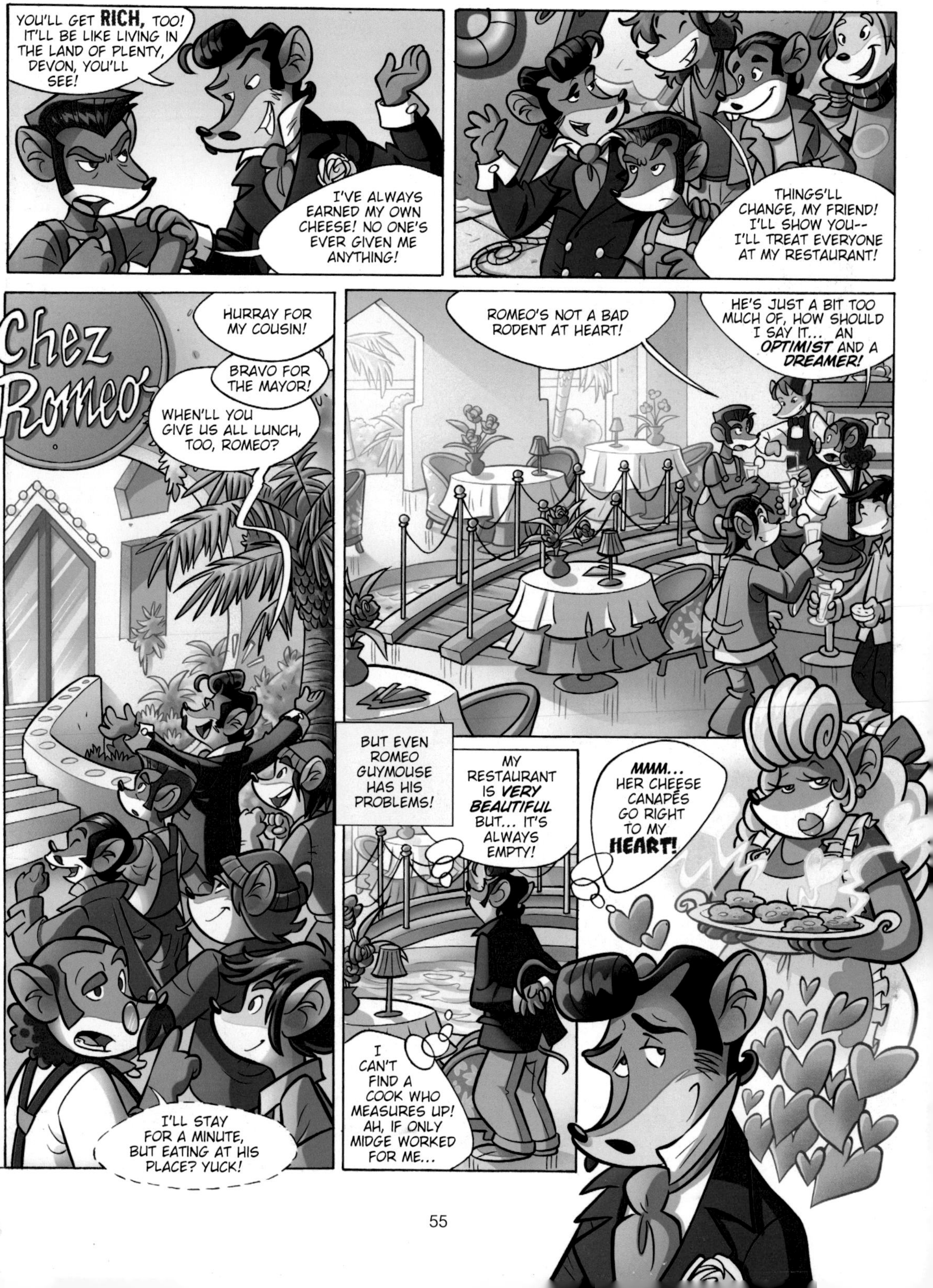
YOU'LL GET RICH, TOO! IT'LL BE LIKE LIVING IN THE LAND OF PLENTY, DEVON, YOU'LL SEE!
I'VE ALWAYS EARNED MY OWN CHEESE! NO ONE'S EVER GIVEN ME ANYTHING!
THINGS'LL CHANGE, MY FRIEND! I'LL SHOW YOU-- I'LL TREAT EVERYONE AT MY RESTAURANT!
Chez Romeo
HURRAY FOR MY COUSIN!
BRAVO FOR THE MAYOR!
WHEN'LL YOU GIVE US ALL LUNCH, TOO, ROMEO?
I'LL STAY FOR A MINUTE, BUT EATING AT HIS PLACE? YUCK!
ROMEO'S NOT A BAD RODENT AT HEART!
HE'S JUST A BIT TOO MUCH OF, HOW SHOULD I SAY IT... AN OPTIMIST AND A DREAMER!
BUT EVEN ROMEO GUYMOUSE HAS HIS PROBLEMS!
MY RESTAURANT IS VERY BEAUTIFUL BUT... IT'S ALWAYS EMPTY!
MMM... HER CHEESE CANAPÉS GO RIGHT TO MY HEART!
I CAN'T FIND A COOK WHO MEASURES UP! AH, IF ONLY MIDGE WORKED FOR ME...

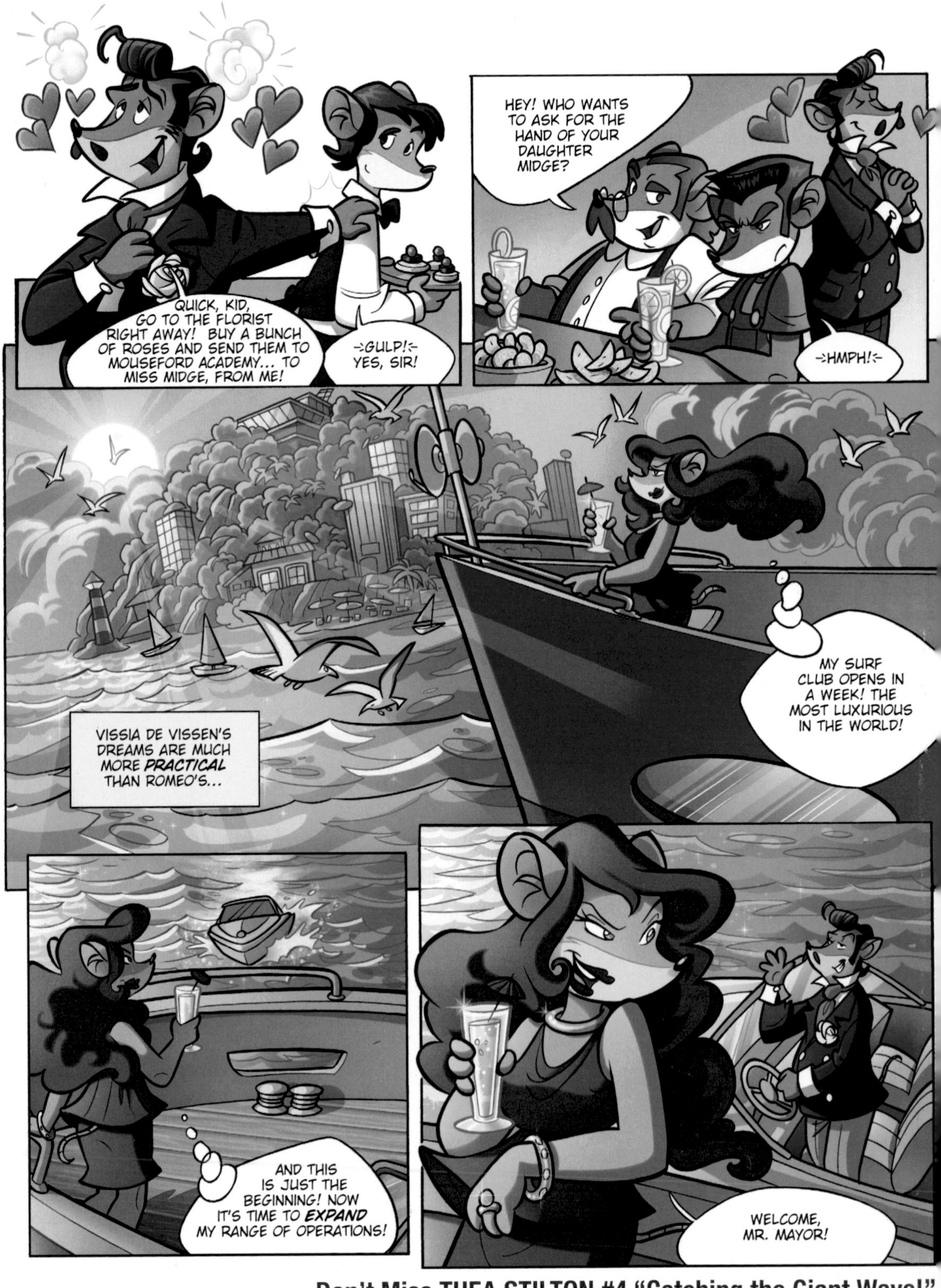
QUICK, KID, GO TO THE FLORIST RIGHT AWAY! BUY A BUNCH OF ROSES AND SEND THEM TO MOUSEFORD ACADEMY... TO MISS MIDGE, FROM ME!
-GULP!- YES, SIR!
HEY! WHO WANTS TO ASK FOR THE HAND OF YOUR DAUGHTER MIDGE?
-HMPH!-
VISSIA DE VISSEN'S DREAMS ARE MUCH MORE PRACTICAL THAN ROMEO'S...
MY SURF CLUB OPENS IN A WEEK! THE MOST LUXURIOUS IN THE WORLD!
AND THIS IS JUST THE BEGINNING! NOW IT'S TIME TO EXPAND MY RANGE OF OPERATIONS!
WELCOME, MR. MAYOR!

Don't Miss THEA STILTON #4 "Catching the Giant Wave!"

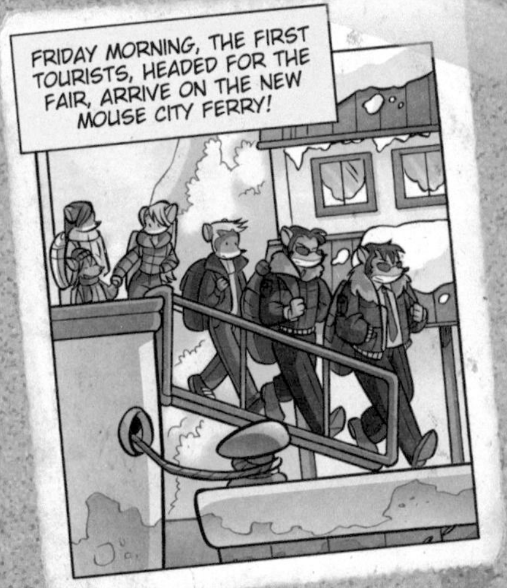
FRIDAY MORNING, THE FIRST TOURISTS, HEADED FOR THE FAIR, ARRIVE ON THE NEW MOUSE CITY FERRY!

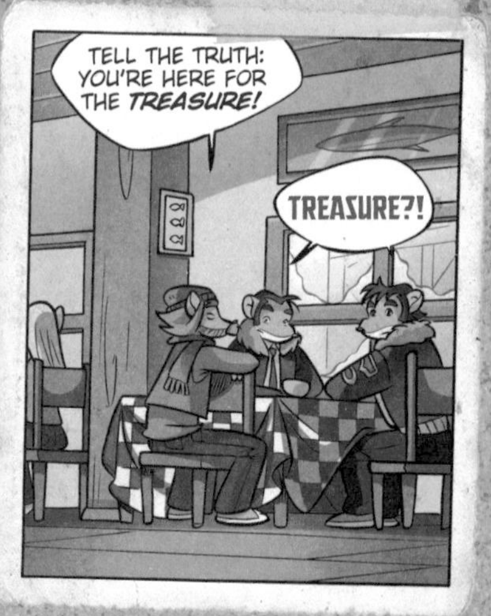
TELL THE TRUTH: YOU'RE HERE FOR THE *TREASURE!*
TREASURE?!

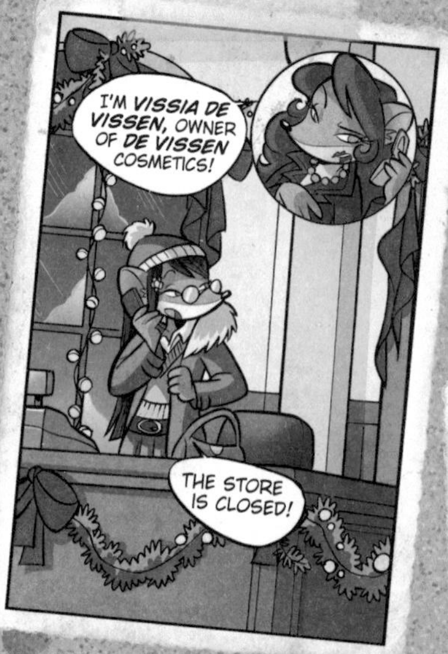
I'M *VISSIA DE VISSEN,* OWNER OF *DE VISSEN* COSMETICS!
THE STORE IS CLOSED!

Chamomile is one of Dina's two sisters. She always seems to have her head in the clouds, but she still manages to come up with the right idea at the right time!

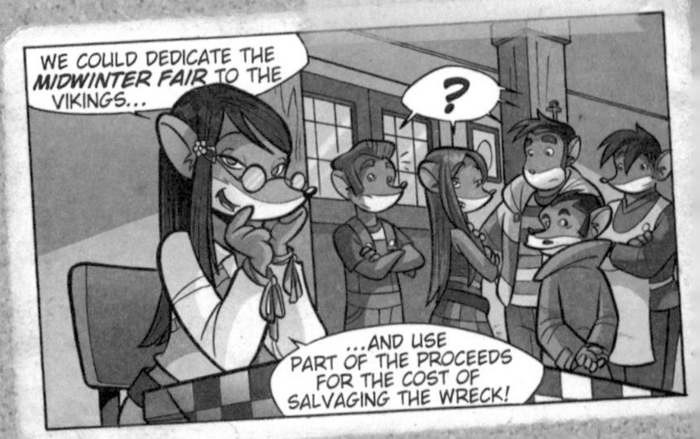
WE COULD DEDICATE THE *MIDWINTER FAIR* TO THE VIKINGS...
?
...AND USE PART OF THE PROCEEDS FOR THE COST OF SALVAGING THE WRECK!

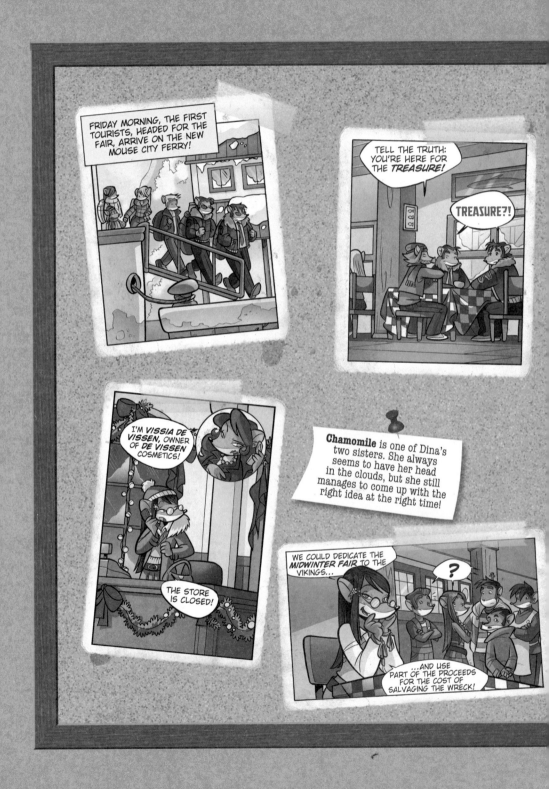